The Valley of Happiness

Published by Raw Dog Screaming Press
Bowie, MD
All rights reserved.
First Edition

"Striper" appeared in *Journal of Curriculum Theorizing*
"Televangelist at the Texas Motel" in *Gulf Coast*
"The Valley of Happiness" and "Wabash" in *Boulevard*
"The Bay of Drake" in *Reed*

Cover: The Magpie on the Gallows painted by Pieter Bruegel the Elder
Book design: Jennifer Barnes

Printed in the United States of America

ISBN: 978-1-935738-67-1

Library of Congress Control Number: 2014952177

www.RawDogScreaming.com

The Valley of Happiness

and other stories by
George Williams

RAW DOG
SCREAMING
PRESS

Acknowledgements

The author thanks Richard Burgin, Neil Sebacher, Edwin Williams, and Eric Miles Williamson, without whose help many of these stories would not have appeared in past or present form. The author also wishes to express his gratitude to the Williams of Archer Street and Sleepy Hollow, the Sebachers of Somersworth, and Corra Films of New York City.

Contents

Striper

Weather permitting, every Saturday before dawn I drove with my fishing buddy Bill to Toledo Bend, the reservoir of the Sabine that, south of Longview, turns into the border of Louisiana and Texas and flows southeast past Dead, Burnt Stump, and Lost Lakes, past Coffee Ground and Old River Coves, and drains into the Gulf of Mexico.

On a Saturday morning in January we launched the boat into the choppy waters and, as was our custom, headed to the Highway 21 Bridge, where schools of striper fed over the mossbeds growing along the underwater pilings. I took a fat water dog out of my Woodstream and impaled it on a shiny new hook. Bill tossed me a cold beer. He dangled a Bass Buster in the air.

No way we don't get a minimum dozen today.

No way.

Against a deep blue sky stacks of fiery cumuli climbed the horizon.

Bill asked, Ever tell you about the time my little wife lifted the side of our house? He was a park ranger who hung around my department. His wife was a powerlifter, in training for the nationals.

No, I said.

Lifted it right up to her belly button. Our dog Spose was trapped under there, you see.

I see.

She made me crawl under there and hold it up, with my back, understand me, while she wiggled between pier and beam looking for the little rascal.

No kidding.

No kidding.

I cast.

Did I ever tell you about the time my son snagged a great white?

Tuesday week, I said. Bill rebaited his hook.

Must have been sixty foot, he said. He was looking sternward toward the shore of the reservoir. I was seated on the bow facing starboard, watching the water.

It weighed near two ton. He opened another beer.

For real.

For real. You know what she did?

The shark?

My wife.

Can't say I do.

Took it down to Angler's Trophy. When I came home from work the next day she had it baked in foil. It sat on the dining room table, looking up at me. It looked lost, or hungry.

How did it taste?

Best shark I ever ate. Know what the taxidermist found? In its gut?

A space ship.

Close.

An astronaut.

Nope.

What?

A gold ingot.

Naa.

Yep, he said. How do you think I bought this bucket?

Bill's cousin had sold it to him for one hundred and fifty dollars. It was battered, and leaky, and smelled, this morning and all the others, like river mud.

I caught a striper. It flapped and shook, dripping, at the end of the line. I threw it back. Bill pitched me another beer. The boat rocked.

We fished. The morning widened. Later the shadows of clouds moved across the water.

I was not a good fisherman, truth to tell, though I liked the sport, to the exclusion of more familiar obligations, like family, job, and friends, with the exception of Bill, whose wife shared too the fate of fishermen's wives.

I had an affinity for underwater creatures, cold-blooded or mammal. I was conceived Italian—my parents are Romans—but my father's side, Delphantia, were generations of sailors from the district of Calabria, the tip of the boot; two months before I was delivered my father was transferred to Houston, Texas, by Agip, Italy's version of Exxon, where I arrived, crying, and there grew up; after graduating from Rice, I moved to San Augustine, where I worked for Texas Wildlife Management as a water analyst, until this fishing trip.

I was born *Corsican*, my mother used to say, with a romantic flourish of her hand; my wife, a native Texan of Anglo-Saxon descent, was born a very creamy white, with undertones of blue, on account of her father's considerable petrochemical fortune, which we stood one day to inherit. Jennifer, however, was impatient. My salary was a modest GS Grade 8, Step 5, Washington approved. It satisfied the bank, which owned everything we claimed to. I refused my father-in-law's help, though I knew Jennifer, without consulting me, did not.

What I enjoyed about fishing was not the angling itself but the vast early morning quiet of the lake—before powerboats swarmed the reservoir—with gentle waves lapping the boat, and the full Coleman cooler of beer, empty by eleven, which signaled the end of the fishing day, as skiers stretched into phosphorescent diving suits, and pulled by Cobra motors, crisscrossed the agitated water, sending arcs of slalom spray over our heads. I taught Bill how to give them the Italian finger.

It was around 8:30, and we hadn't had a nibble in minutes.

No way we're not going to snag two dozen this morning.

No way.

My line twitched, then yanked with such violence I was nearly thrown from the boat. The pole bent to break.

Jesus Christ, Bill said.

The boat rocked and hit one of the pilings. Empties rolled. I let out line, then reeled it in.

Help, I said.

Bill stepped unsteadily over the cooler. I secured my grip and pulled. With his net Bill hauled in a striper.

It must weigh a hundred pounds, he said. The bass flopped between the two seats. Its tail knocked over the cooler. I splashed water on the fish.

What are you doing?

It'll die.

Bill took an oar and smacked its head.

9

That's the point.

It stopped moving, just like that.

You killed it, I said.

You're welcome, he said. I had a momentary impulse to stave in his skull with the anchor.

Let's go home.

At the landing fishermen marveled at the catch. Within ten minutes a newspaper reporter from Lufkin was on his way out with a photographer. My picture was taken with the beautiful striper.

After the interview the reporter told me he was a member of the Sierra Club.

Why did you kill it? he asked. A beautiful, rare fish. One in a billion. I looked for his eyes behind sunglasses.

I didn't, I said, and cut Bill a look. It died in the net. Could have never brought it in otherwise. Line too weak. Snap.

At home that afternoon I wrapped the fish in foil and lowered it gently into the giant freezer in the garage.

My wife framed my picture. She decided to invite a dozen friends over for a fry.

Fried bass? I felt uneasy about the fish, I couldn't say why.

All week at work the striper was on my mind. It was such a marvel. National Geographic wanted to take measurements. Later that evening my wife said a team of ichthyologists from the Smithsonian would be flying down Monday.

I guess we won't eat it.

Of course not, my wife said, in a tone that reminded me that I was predictably stupid about the ways of her world. She was chopping a head of cabbage.

We'll sell it. Their taxidermists will mount it. Your name will be in the Smithsonian. She tossed the shredded head into a glass bowl.

No kidding.

Addie said we ought to have an auction. Addie was Jennifer's sister, a year older.

For a fish?

She had a face lift last week.

At twenty-nine?

Is that too young? It's not like she can't afford it.

Addie had married a Houston lawyer ten years her senior, the newest partner in a major firm that specialized in environmental law. Their corporate client list was a mile long.

Whose idea was it? I meant the auction, but she misunderstood.

Her allergies get worse every year. Ragweed, mold spores. He said her eyes were always puffy.

Next he'll want her to have breast implants.

How did you know?

Friday night I took the striper out of the freezer and put it on my worktable. The next morning in the darkness of pre-dawn I was walking through the garage when I heard a sigh.

I turned around. Beneath the layers of coldness the striper was moving faintly. It looked at me and blinked.

Help, it said.

In the bedroom I ripped the electric blanket off the bed.

What? my wife said. She sat up.

The fish, I said. It's talking.

Oh. She fell back on the bed.

I warmed the bass and put it in a wheelbarrow and rolled it into the backyard to my son's aluminum pool, which I filled with a garden hose.

The fish swam around, contented.

Every so often it surfaced.

Thank you, it said.

You're welcome, I said.

Later it said, Perhaps you're wondering who I am.

No, I said.

Well, in any case, my name is Federigo. Fred, if you like. After millennia, after the ice age and continental drifts, I wind up in a dreary man-made Texas reservoir. It was passable until the invention of racing boats. Observe.

The fish—Fred I mean—swam backwards and turned around. Down its back ran the path of a lacerating propeller.

Ouch, I said.

Gizmo prop. Unbridled fiends. Furthermore, banks ought not to approve so many boat loans. Whenever I hear those noisy contraptions I head to the bottom of the lake.

I don't blame you.

You must be a man of breeding, not to possess one.

I can't afford one.

Get another job, the fish said, smiling.

I fed Fred the salamanders for the morning trip. When Bill honked at the end of the drive, I walked out into the smoky dawn and explained to him I was feeling somewhat insane, and not up to fishing this morning.

He laughed.

See you tonight, then.

Right, I said, remembering the fry, then remembered it was off. It was too late. Bill sped away in his Bronco. I watched his taillights round the curve. A beer can flew out the window.

I poured whiskey in my coffee. In the bathroom I said my name two or three times in front of the mirror, to make sure.

What do you want? I asked the fish.

Nothing, it said.

I could not think for the longest while.

Wait here.

In my study I took my solar-powered calculator and two boxes of bills from the file drawer of my desk. I figured my net worth to be -$245,678 and 43 cents. My wife and I, as we had grown accustomed to accept, had a routinized life, while both of us, without daring to speak the truth, looked forward to inheriting her family fortune, which would somehow change everything. My son was deaf and blind from TV, and dumb as far as I could tell, since he rarely spoke. Why did I like to fish so much?

I stood beside the pool.

Wincing, crying, I flopped onto the lawn.

Not yet, I said.

I proposed a plan.

I put the blanket back on my wife. I looked in on my son. The tiny TV sunk into his pillows glowed at him. He slept with foam earphones on. His Power

Rangers t-shirt was snot-stained. I kissed him good-bye. His face twitched, like a fly had landed on his nose.

I drove to Lake Texoma and dropped off the striper.

Hey Fred, I said, thanks. And don't forget my wife.

A big polished boat of bass fishers looked our way. They watched the fish swim.

Boy, one said.

To Fred I said, Tell them to kiss my dago ass.

Kiss his ass, Fred said, and swam away.

Shoot, a fisherman said, he *painted* them stripes on.

Right, I said. I gave them the Italian fist.

My wife would wish for money. I would soon be forgotten, thank God.

I drove to the Dallas airport and took a flight through New York to Rome, where I boarded a train for the tip of the peninsula, admiring the land where my forefathers lived and died for a thousand years.

I got off at Melito di Porto Salvo. I walked to the beach facing the Straight of Messina.

Sunbathers lay on the white blinding sand, a sheen like delicious sex on their brown bodies. The water was clear blue. The women were topless.

I stripped. I had a tremendous erection. A sunbather screamed.

I unwrapped the large vanity mirror I bought in Rome and set it in the sand. Now, I said.

In a momentary agony of metamorphosis, I fell onto the warm beach, my diminished hands webbed into flippers. I looked into the mirror. I was the most beautiful oceanic dolphin I had ever seen. Bottlenosed, with the finely intelligent face of a child. I squeaked with pleasure.

A sunbather, standing up to flee, fainted.

I flopped and rocked back and forth to the foamy surf. A wave rolled up and I rode it into the sea.

I lost consciousness of time, but for what must have been months I explored the watery depths of the Mediterranean with a friendly school of dolphins headed for Cyprus. The smiling mammals took me in like a lost soul, and treated me with respect, though I think they thought I was paralyzed with fright—or brain damaged—from being caught in a Japanese tuna net, since I could not communicate intelligibly with any of the group, and had to be shown how to navigate, and what to eat.

One day in the Ionian Sea I vanished from my own sight. I woke to a terrified face. At the end of a bed, propped up by pillows, and wearing a pair of half-glasses, my wife sat holding a folded section of the *Houston Chronicle*. She was screaming. I rolled off the bed onto the floor, terrified that in paroxysms of disbelief she would find a desperate means of hurting me. During the confusion I took note of the fact that my wife appeared no older than nineteen.

Trembling violently, she punched 0 on the bedside phone.

The two policemen she ushered into the bedroom were at a considerable loss, though they assumed, for the moment, a professional indifference towards the indisputable fact that an eight-hundred-pound oceanic dolphin soaked in saltwater, with seaweed tangled around its dorsal fin, rocked back and forth on the plush orange Wear-Dated shag piles of a Lufkin suburban bedroom, one hundred and twenty miles from the nearest inhabitable body of water. One officer, apparently a rookie, volunteered to shoot the trespasser, and leave it at that.

His partner waved him away.

Explain what happened again, ma'am. My wife hugged herself.

I was in bed reading, she said, when I looked up and discovered this *thing* at my feet.

Go on.

That's all.

That's it? the rookie asked.

You sure you didn't fall asleep? the other office asked, silencing his partner with a raised hand.

What *fucking* difference does it make?

I recognized an attitude.

The rookie blushed. I heard the sound of a video game my son was playing in the den. It was midnight.

Maybe a suspect, the other said, brushing his badge with the back of his hand, entered the premises with the object in question while you were unawares.

14

Obviously. Her eyes welled up. But I wasn't asleep. I was reading an article about a man who disappeared and assumed a new identity in another state. No one found out until he was killed in a car accident.

How's that?

I was wishing my goddamn husband would come home. Or at least his body turn up.

Sorry ma'am, the older officer said. He tipped the brim of his blue hat.

I flopped up and down, crying desperately, laughing.

The rookie drew his gun.

It's a *porpoise*, his partner said.

My wife moved to her dressing chair.

It must be a practical joke, she said.

Do you have any known enemies? the rookie asked.

Hundreds, she said. I watched the young officer stare at her flawless cleavage in the mirror. He took out a note pad.

I know this is a difficult time, he said, but we'll need for you to give us their names. My wife smiled for the other officer.

Could you please take away the fish?

I was put in my son's pool. The next day two trainers from Sea World rounded the piney drive in a van. Through the den window I watched them speak with my wife. They all shook hands. My son came out and poked me with a stick.

I was taken to Sea World and lowered into the giant tank with several other dolphins, ignorant as I, their captivity rendering them dumb as dinosaurs, though they were receptive to my signals, which I had mastered in the Mediterranean. Within days I mounted an insurrection. Following my example, the other dolphins refused to jump through hoops or perform ridiculous tricks for stale fish. I was considered a bad influence, so the keepers lifted me with a crane and dropped me into a smaller tank, where alone I was watched by thousands and thousands of tourists passing silently before the thick glass, who occasionally rapped the pane, in desperate hope believing they were communicating with a superior intelligence. Their mournful optimism depressed the hell out of me.

One day I looked up and saw my wife and son. It was Saturday. They waved. I waved back. They moved with the crowd out of sight. Every six months or so they appeared, and moved on.

Once a trainer accidentally dropped an employee manual into my tank. I pretended to read it, turning pages with my flipper. It became a motif. They submerged a recliner and a reading lamp. During a special ceremony I was given a stack of waterproofed Harvard Classics donated by the San Antonio Public Library. My photograph was taken with an underwater actor impersonating Einstein. I became the symbol for a national literacy campaign sponsored by the First Lady.

One Sunday Bill passed before the glass with his powerlifter spouse. They were arguing. Her mouth accused him of sleeping with Jennifer. His mouth said they had screwed one another's brains out, so what.

She decked him with a right cross. He was out cold.

I swam in circles. I could not stop laughing.

One day my wife and son appeared, with a man I did not recognize. He put his arm around her. I read her lips. She told him the story about the dolphin appearing at the foot of her bed, leaving out important details of course, but he enjoyed the yarn just the same. I gave them both the finger.

At night I read *The Odyssey*, or Ovid. The literacy stint is growing tiresome. Every day I wait for the trainer to drop a can of beer into the aquarium. I want to go fishing, alone.

Ghostly

After Mass I explained my problem to the monsignor in his rectory office.

Could you drop by my house soon? I was desperate. I hadn't slept in days. I was Catholic then.

Tonight.

He leaned back in his padded chair and tossed a dart over my head at a corkboard. He missed.

Sure, he said. Like some, he never looked at me for long, if at all.

Father, I said, do you think Satan is working his will in contemporary America?

Who?

Do you think my house is haunted by a demon?

Do you watch television?

No.

Probably not. What's your advertising profile?

Excuse me?

Age, sex, race, religion, employment, education, political orientation, et cetera.

Forty-two. Male. Texan. Democrat. Latin and history instructor, high school. M.A.—

Small fry. If it's a demon, it's been sent to force you out of your house. You know, get you to drive around, shop, spend your disposable income, fill you with envy, make you long for a car phone. As a teacher your social credibility is so low advertisers don't even bother. You're down there with senators and sex killers.

You mean, if I were filled with cupidity and spent all my money the demon would leave my house?

Well, he'd possess *you* then, now wouldn't he?

The priest laughed and threw another dart.

Emblazoned on the corkboard was the omnipresent and jaundiced *Smile!* face which had plagued my native land for so long, and driven many to self-immolation, as they felt in their hearts and souls little mirth, dying every day in the dragonish climate of their country, though they did not recognize that they were dying, but felt obliged to grin like skulls whenever they ventured (fearful of their sanity every step of the way) into tremendous and labyrinthine shopping bazaars, to exchange whatever obscenity a relative had purchased in these polished tombs, where specters called *consumers* drifted for days, losing their way in agonies of indecision, transfixed by the soft breezes of narcotizing melodia of these vast gallerias, overwhelmed, then stupefied by the infinite variety of useless products that multiplied before their eyes.

I suffered at the hands of this mall insanity, once. I was returning to *Sears* department store a pair of studded leatherette swimwear my shy nine-year-old niece had given me for Christmas, with a violent pink sleeveless t-shirt on which was printed HOT U ME, when the clerk, having argued for a half an hour about the sale price of the garment, implied that I was trying to swindle the plunderbund by returning obviously second-hand feathers. Deeply wounded by this accusation (I had used tongs to lift the salacious habits back into the box after they had leapt out at me, a nest of snakes), I replied, You may have them back, sir, in exchange for nothing, but if you ever again condemn my character by accusing me of such conduct, I will be obliged to drive a stake through your heart. He smiled, baring his fangs. When he said, Have a good weekend—or was it, Have a nice day? I cannot remember, perhaps he said, *Taddy a woody bebush*, but it was the *way* he intoned this mantra that nearly snapped the thin cord that tethers ghost to bone—I seized a can of lighter fluid from the counter of a tobacco shop adjoining PASSION BODS, aside YEARNING TOTS, and, dousing my chest, set myself on fire. In a fit of psychoreactive depression caused by a chemical imbalance, I was told by a psychiatrist.

I woke in a hospital ward, where I remained for three months. My face, I was relieved to see, was more or less unaltered, except for the left side. My neck was scarred significantly. I will not, I cannot, describe the oceanic swirls of disfigured flesh I have grown to admire and still refer to as my chest.

Oops, the priest said, grinning.

I turned around. The dart he'd just thrown was harpooned on a crucifix, above a shelf of golfing trophies.

When in Rome, he said. He looked spookily around the room and laughed. I felt the skin on my skull crawl to and fro.

Are you a drinker? he asked.

Medium. You?

Heavy.

That night Monsignor and I sat in my living room and drank a bottle of Old Weller. At first nothing happened, except Monsignor's nose reddened. It looked like a beaker of blood. For a blessed hour we heard no flatulent sighs, Pig Latin, or eructations, as I had cautioned him to tune his ears to witness.

I was at the sideboard pouring another drink, when the ghost thrashed the monsignor about the face with invisible fists. The priest fell back on the sofa, already stunned by the bourbon. He staggered to his car and returned with a young woman, Diana by name, a girl I recognized as the lay leader of the weekly folk Mass I routinely avoided, since its noise depressed me.

Diana carried a Stratocaster and a small Fender amplifier. She smiled at me, and softly blushed. She was embarrassed by my ugliness.

You poor man, she asked, what happened to your face?

Gin blossoms, the monsignor said, taking a pull off the bottle.

I fell asleep at the beach, I said. We all laughed.

She was tall, a striking girl, with delicate brunette ringlets of hair that fell to her shoulders, with a face possessed of a winsome smile, and a body whose configuration I confess I immediately imagined beneath her strapless sundress. It was Whit Sunday. She arranged her equipment, then stood on the sofa.

Watch this, the priest said.

The events which followed, and in what order, I cannot with complete accuracy recollect, as I was dazed with drink—and amazement—but I believe them to have unfolded in the following manner.

Pausing before she commenced plucking the detestable sound machine, she took an aerosol can out of her purse, and spraying what I reckoned to be shaving cream onto her palm, greased her hair and provoked it like crazy knives and coils of barbed wire, after which astonishing transfiguration she jolted my heart by suddenly ripping and stripping herself of adornments, revealing herself to be wearing only a ruffled pink string which ran down her *mons veneris* and up the valley of her buttocks and around her perfect waist. Her nipples were like nails and glowed in the light of their ideal angulation. She stroked the instrument, lasciviously fretting its neck, from which devilish invention a cacophony unknown to historical man issued forth, all the while gyrating and undulating obscenely on my chesterfield. I looked at the priest in horror. He was visibly excited.

Then what few men could survive to tell took place before my unbelieving eyes. Strumming maniacal and chordless twangs from the hellish board of wires, she squeezed her succulent breast—left side, if I remember correctly—so perfectly formed, so rare, and so much in her hand like a beautifully leashed beast, that I nearly fell to my knees for succor. As if fire issued forth, the ghost shrieked, and whirled around the room, knocking over lamps, turning over furniture, hurling knickknacks from the whatnots, screaming *Kyrie Kyrie Kyrie* and, finally, burnt to an invisible crisp, smashed through the picture window overlooking a strip-mine of shopping centers, pizza franchises, and video chains and, howling into the vasty deep of the night sky, vanished from my house forever.

I fainted. When I came to, the priest and the girl (now clothed and again demur) were discussing dates in the monsignor's appointment book.

City Hall tomorrow, the monsignor said.

Then Fillmore High, she reminded the priest.

Dear Lord yes, he said, reminded.

Am I dreaming? I asked.

Partly, the monsignor said, draining the whiskey bottle. But console yourself with this. By the mercy of God you have been spared.

From what?

The priest laughed.

Drink, I said.

He handed me the dead soldier, and left. The room smelled like burnt hair.

I saw Diana again, though not in church, as I never again stepped foot on the parish grounds, fearful of her gift of exorcism, and terrified of the beauty of her breasts, though I was reminded of the event every Sunday, when the electronic bells sounding from the spire of the church made me so mindful of the event I nearly lost my sanity. I sold my house and moved across town.

20

I encountered both the priest and the ghost again, separately, on more than one occasion.

I was returning from the grocery store when, several cars ahead of me, a truck filled with hydrochloric acid jackknifed, spilling its contents on the road. The steel-belted radials on my Lumina exploded, then melted. I swerved to avoid a downed motorcyclist, whose leather jacket was steaming from the fuming solution. I pulled over and removed the gas mask from the glove compartment. Foolishly in my panic I stepped out to aid the now dancing and prancing biker, who could not find a shore safe from the deluge. He cried out in a panic of disbelief at his own dissolving person. My shoes melted. I climbed back in my car and locked the doors. I watched the misfortuned cyclist disappear in an agony reminiscent of the Wicked Witch of the West's grand finale. Then the road disappeared in a haze of chemical smoke. The car sank into the softened asphalt. For the first time in years I prayed for my safety.

The ghost, in the car, where it had hidden, I sensed, since the night Diana exorcized it with her fields of lily, said, Coward, and tweaked my gas mask. It flew through the roof and disappeared.

The Hazardous Materials unit screamed onto the scene. All of us, except the biker, were saved. On the evening news, which I watched in my favorite bar, the anchor, whose face can only be described as a Rottweiler's, wrapped up his report of the boy's death significantly by informing the public the victim had not been wearing his seat belt, nor a helmet, nor had he registered with the Selective Service.

The next morning on the front seat of my car I found a calling card. On it were embossed the words *Caligula's, Gentlemen's Club and Cabaret.* Written in childish hand in the bottom corner was the capital letter *D*.

I ironed a white shirt and wore a tie bearing my family heraldry, an armory most beautifully composed of a black *wappen* with an ermine bordure, a manly helmet of argent, with a crest purpure, potent mantling, and pean supportings. The shield itself is an extraordinary achievement of chevrons and piles.

At the club I was forced to pay twenty dollars for entree. A gorgeous woman, possessed of a throaty voice, sat provocatively half disrobed in a booth above a softly spotlit stage, where, as music jockey, she selected the records and announced the next stripteuse who would grace the gentlemen by crawling, swinging, shaking, climbing, and otherwise doing extraordinary gymnastics with the limbey meekness of denuded beauty, in order to reveal to the men what they already knew, but who must have their suspicions confirmed nonetheless, again and again, it appeared, as the place was packed, that women are more beautiful than men, and the most the hapless men can do is yearn, pitched to and fro on drunken boats cast on the blue sea of unbearable erotic exhalations of linctures, morphias, tinctures of lotus and opium, driven down rivers of Lethe, encircled by the physics of sleep in the metamorphic form of dancing girls, with not a drop of sleep to drink.

The woman spoke smokily into a large and unfortunately angled microphone.

Gentlemen, you will not believe your eyes, you will not believe your eyes. All rise for the anthem. I offer you Diana. Look at this goddess, gentlemen, look at this goddess of your dreamy dreams.

I looked up. To a low wail of a song made sweeter and slower by the sadness of my heart, she stepped from behind a white column lowered *deus ex machina* onto the stage, where she allowed her white silken night dress to whisper down her waist, where the space that triangulates—thigh to honey to thigh—was the most perfectly shaped the audience had ever witnessed (they sighed the moment she revealed her *mons veneris*), and turning around, bent over slightly, to show to the world of what ideal place, at what splendid angle, the Creator had placed her kitty. Slowly she stepped out of the muss of silk delicately chaining her ankles, her figure a sea-foam of perfection washed to the widened shores of my eyes. She wore black heels, which served to excite the patrons even more, as if that were necessary, or desirable, which businessmen approached her in polite droves, gently snapping her blue and pink g-string of white airy wedges of lace, cuneiform of her universal tongue, receiving her soft busses on their ears, bending to admire the erotic symmetries which threatened to drive them mad, and offer her a dollar, which bills she strung around her waist until she looked like Diana herself, goddess not merely of the moon, but of the woodland, goddess of the hunt, wearing a loincloth of leaves, so I choose to see it, as the fact that she moved so catlike, so cannily around the stage, one minute on all fours, the next standing up tall, arching up, reaching up, then down—she approached six feet in heels— deliriously intoxicated by the beauty of her own body as she uplifted and admired her perfect configurations, first one, then the other, dancing in front of the wall of mirrors that encased the stage, a crystal palace of pleasures, the fact that she was not veiled in woodland beauty, leaves of magnolia, dogwood, cypress, cinnamon, chestnut, rosewood, witch hazel, juniper, buttonwood, acacia, rain tree, nutmeg, ginkgo, poplar, mountain lilac, but strung up, trussed, strapped with cash, plastered with lucre, grey scabrous tender, filled me with an overwhelming desire to weep, which temptation I resisted, for I have not ever, nor probably ever will, shed a tear when I am in a condition I can only describe as erect.

She was doubtless the most desired angel in the establishment. To my relief, no invisible fires issued forth, though the degree of infatuation the businessmen displayed for far too long, in my opinion, made me pray she might blind them in the manner she banished the ghost from my house.

One poor gentleman, finely attired, fell to his knees and began kissing her feet, just where patent leather formed its border with the barely visible cleavage of her toes. A security guard appeared out of nowhere and knocked the delirious gynomaniac unconscious with a nightstick and dragged him out a side door. When I returned to my car the poor reveler, already tormented by beauty, lay unconscious under a boxwood, where two low born patrons urinated on his back of pin-strips.

I waited in my car until closing, when Diana left by the back door and drove west in her Mercedes on the interstate, stopping at a Hilton beside a shopping mall. I parked and waited, uncertain of my approach, and how I might explain to her the divine and charitable love I felt in my heart and soul for her entire being, which I would pledge to honor and obey until death does us part.

The desk clerk informed me that Ms. Johnson had checked into room 1265, and wished not to be disturbed until ten a.m.

I requested and received room 1267. The bellhop eyed me suspiciously, as I had no luggage, but I tipped the miserable man a quarter nevertheless. The ingrate scowled.

I hesitated before Diana's door, fearful my interruption would not initiate a harmonious relationship between our ardent souls, but rather make her believe I was headstrong, impatient, and merely in desire of suckle about her extraordinary breasts, which I confess I was, though only in the proper context of marital relations of mutual respect and connubial happiness, candid and easeful, with moral decency, and most importantly spontaneous affection, at least ten times a day, I figured we were worthy of.

In the dark of my room I paced and smoked and drank occasionally from a bottle of Old Weller, 107 proof, which it is my habit to carry everywhere I go in this dangerous Texas town.

At three a.m. I pulled a chair out onto the balcony, which overhung a strip of fajita chains and adult bookstores. I smoked, drowsing in the chair, awaiting my hour of truth.

I was startled awake by a beastly noise whose source confused me. Instantly to my feet, I leaned around the partition that separates the balconies. Through the sliding glass door I saw a scene of such indescribable horror I can barely bring myself to testify. A waxing moon was rising. I reckoned it was five a.m.

Kneeling on the floor, and without a shred of nightdress on her heavenly body, my beloved Diana was performing in a state of dismaying urgency, acts of fiendish delight on brute red manhoods, some surprisingly tiny, others considerably larger (I have only my own to judge by) attached to seven of the businessmen I had seen ogling her sacred woodlands the night before.

The monsignor, bottle in hand, staggered around the bed, blessing this service, and laughing.

Some of the merchants had approached high tide; others were ebbing, though still quite interested, as the look in their eyes was so entirely animal I was not certain they were not possessed of horny skulls. String swung from her chin and sickly whey streamed down her face like ribbons of tears and dripped onto her breasts, resting on her chest like pearls, spotting her wanton tresses of dark waving hair like viscous diamonds. Another businessman was copulating with her as if she were a dog, whose grunts were the source of my surprise as I waited for the sun to sweeten the day of my proposal, as each businessman jettisoned his fury of lickerish, profaning her holy image, as if each in his own masturbatic rapture, so practiced, so knowledged, so utterly and willfully mired in the loathsome dungbag of the homo habilis corpus, held by their dark lights her extraordinary beauty in absolute contempt, and forked over a thousand dollar bill for the favor of hating her.

The men cheered one another on. Denuded of all but their ostrich boots, I recognized these Huns as oil executives.

What metaphors the whoremasters used to describe such concourse I am not morally bound to report, as the phrases were so heinous my ears burn with shame, and my heart brims with retributive humors, when I recollect for what they had the arrogance and unmanliness and spiritual ignorance to compare the acts they were perpetrating on my fiancé *to*. I urge you not to imagine these tropes, as part of your soul will die, gangrenous of the pit, where the Great Satan snatches ravening toothfuls out of the rotting souls of the unbridled, debauched ruts of Cephisus and offspring of Onan, ejactomaniacal oilmen, who, fearless of God's displeasure, void their ithyphallic curd on the numinous Artemis Angelorum *de die in diem*, goddess of this wracked planet, procreant of the world, ever more a sea of black gumbos drawn from the bowels of the dimming globe, laughing as he laps their coagulate blood elixed with Pennzoils and sebums sucked from the molten depths of eternal darkness, hateful nards, bilious glycerins, black waxes, oleaginous ejecta, nauseous ravens of tar, sulphurs of naphthylamine smuts and gummy soots, gnashing their oily animi in the howl of eternal whirlwinds.

I watched for what seemed like an hour. Now sated with innumerable turns subjugating my beloved exorcist with freshets (where, rubbing the bemonstered oblatives as if they were the cool of salubrious oils, emollients pressed from an otherworldly flower—when in fact with their pyrognostic hexane propellants, distillations of the underworld petroleum, dark tallow siphoned from the inferno's rivers of fire, she unknowingly scorched her skin—burns not visible but to the eyes of my soul—and moaned as if the malicious, blistering resins were a sustenance without which her person was in mortal peril), the executives showered and dressed. In front of the dresser mirror they adjusted their wigs and blowdried their hair and flexed their obscene musculatures, and, grimacing like vain apes through false teeth and surgically drawn chins, left the hotel room, smiling with hateful satisfaction at their humiliation of the beautiful Diana, now smutched by their vile concupiscence. I prayed beloved Artemis would transform these lascivious oilmen into baldfaced stags, who, screaming, wake to find their dungbag bodies devoured by hound dogs, white-collar Actaeons ground into Alpo.

The priest took his cut and left.

Alone now, naked, plastered with the viscosities of those devils, and looking suddenly very weary, Diana too showered, and returned in a white robe to calculate her earnings. She took a pistol from her purse, and, walking to the balcony, from which side I withdrew my startled face, stood at the railing and pointed the gun at the parking lot. She pulled the trigger seven times. The gun was unloaded. With each *click* she informed her clients they had better fuck themselves very soon, or she would be obliged to fuck them up, with lead.

It was Monday prime.

I knew then I was smitten forever. I leapt over to her balcony, and, falling to my knees, poured out my heart and soul into the folds of her robe.

You are burned, I cried, burned, scorched as I am. The ghost in the room blessed us. She was the only one who had asked about my face. Many stared, others looked away, angry and ashamed, or pretended not to notice, when I showed them the hideous side, sometimes deliberately.

We were married within the month but divorced the same year, as I could not persuade her to abandon her chosen profession, or her church music—though she agreed to sever all relations with the priest—nor could I afford to keep her in the style of luxury to which her trade had accustomed her. Usually her night's earnings were spent by the following afternoon on beautiful raiment, sophisticated appliances, and home furnishings from the finest department stores in Texas. I am a schoolteacher, and could only afford to give her the carnations and roses I grew in my garden. When I asked for a divorce, she caressed my disfigured chest and stroked my face, uncomprehending of the fact that I could no longer bear the thought of her folk music accompanying the Mass, nor the image of my wife committing acts of dark congress with bedeviled men, fancy men of rapine, for whom no punishment was issued by the gods for violating her sanctuary, wolfen fishermen angling in her woodland spring which by the power of their malignancy metamorphosed her living waters into lakes of flaming darkness, where dead oil boys, immersed in pits of creosote, lift up their eyes to Abraham and cry, *let Lazarus dip the tip of his finger in water, and cool my tongue, for I am tormented in the flame,* despite the fact she degraded herself for money, and held the beasts in unchecked contempt.

Not enough, I said, grieving that I had no choice but to play the tyrant, for I could truly no longer bear her nightly absence, and what images that returned, as I sat with my bottle of Old Weller, smoking, I am under no obligation to convey.

I felt sorry for you, she said.

So did I. Forgive me. And please, if you love me, go away.

I have not seen her since, though at night visions of sweetness and pain rise to my consciousness like vapors from the deep. I drink and smoke, waiting for the sun to rise, and prepare my classroom curriculum. One cannot read, or understand—or teach—history and expect restorative deep sleep ever again, just as one cannot be happily married and have one's spouse remain a slave to a profession, regardless of its nature.

Last week I saw the priest in street clothes at an A.A. meeting, where he directed prayers and took collection. All of us sat around lunchroom tables. The priest did not recognize me.

You are new here, he said, holding out a wicker basket lined with felt, looking away, trying not to stare.

I threw in a nickel.

You must ask God's forgiveness.

Everyone in the room looked at me, waiting.

God forgive me.

The priest bent down.

You must kneel down and ask.

Kneel?

Yes.

I stood up.

Humble yourself, my son. Pride—

I kicked him in the crotch.

The monsignor fell, flinging the wicker basket into the air. Dimes and quarters rained down on the linoleum floor. People slapped their feet over rolling coins.

Where's Diana? I asked.

Don't, he said. His lips were blue. He got to his knees.

I reared back my leg. Where is she?

He flinched. Married.

Who?

The monsignor fell forward and covered his face.

The Mass, he said, has ended.

I left by the back door. In the car the ghost said, Happy hour. At a drive-thru liquor store I bought a case of Old Weller and a carton of Camels. Home, I boarded up my house from the inside.

Dummy

My inner child woke me up early.

It's time, he said, we made some easy money.

I didn't care for the tone of his voice. It sounded like a threat.

Any bright ideas?

Pimp your wife out to thieves.

We're divorced.

Blackmail a politician.

Again?

Rob a bank.

Lotteries are legal.

Stick up a savings and loan. Federal insurance.

We can play slot machines in Las Vegas, Atlantic City. Blackjack on a gambling cruise from Galveston.

Rob a convenience store.

All right! Just let me sleep.

Or an armored car.

When I woke up my inner child sat on the bed cradling a pistol-grip shotgun. He loaded it.

Where did you get that?

Gun show.

You paid for it?

He pulled a revolver from his Raiders jacket. A gob of fifties fell out of his pocket.

I peeked through the blinds the way an escaped felon in a television movie keeps an eye out from his roadside motel room, because, as an escaped felon in a roadside motel room, I felt I had little say in the matter of how to conduct myself. Could it be helped if the law had already decided (without my consent) that I was indeed guilty of this or that or the other? Didn't I feel too I had the *right* to look through the blinds the way an escaped felon in a television movie keeps an eye out from his roadside motel room, having earned it by escaping from the federal penitentiary in Huntsville in the back of a garbage truck filled with garbage and having spent 24.97 (plus 6 percent for the state, 2 percent for the county, 7 percent for the city, and 2 percent for the Sports Authority, gifts to the governor, commissioners, mayor, and Chairman of the Board from a former prisoner) for a roadside motel room with a television not only without major cable but with snowy reception? Moreover, I enjoyed peeking through the blinds. An attractive woman in a swimsuit—seashells, three strings—walked by carrying a bucket of ice. Physically attractive, I mean. I didn't have time to reach any other conclusions. A shotgun blast exploded my pillow. Stale foam flew everywhere.

Damn, my inner child said, this is *fun*. In her flip flops the woman rounded the corner, spilling ice.

We drove around town looking for an unsuspecting establishment to stick up.

Bank, or convenient store?

Brink's.

Forget it.

Flip.

I tossed a coin.

Heads you lose, my inner child said.

At the convenience store I parked by the pumps. My inner child filled a two-liter Coke bottle with gas and stuffed a rag in its mouth.

Aren't you going to pay for it, I asked.

I've already paid for it. I've paid and paid and paid for it. I'm not paying any more. I'm done paying. It's time to get paid.

You're a criminal and a psychopath, I said. You don't get paid. You thieve, burgle, rob. Sack and pillage. Lay waste. Defile shrill-shrieking daughters. Spit naked infants on pikes. Cut their grandfathers' throats.

I learned this in the Marines, my inner child said.

Like hell you did.

He lit the rag and threw the bottle. It bounced off the store window and rolled off the sidewalk.

My inner child unhooked a nozzle.

Watch this.

An arc of fire shot halfway to the storefront.

Like the devil taking a piss, my inner child said.

A man with a burning newspaper ran back into the store.

Best try another.

Can't we watch?

No more pyrotechnics.

Say what?

If we are going to rob a store we ought not set it ablaze first.

I thought you enjoyed setting fires.

My inner child sobbed.

All right! But no people.

What if they won't get out of the way?

They will.

Frogs?

Absolutely not.

My inner child bawled. Give me the unqualified love you were denied as a child! Indulge me!

I was abused when *I* was a child. *My* parents are toxic! You got that, you ten-dollar piece of plastic shit? You're just a doll that *represents* my inner child. *I'm* the one with the problems here.

You're not my Pa?

No.

Are you my mother?

Negative.

Can I get my tongue pierced?

My inner child, sonny boy, whippersnapper, young buck, wanted most of all to be a holy terror.

31

Let's get laid, he said.

You're a minor.

You're not.

We waited in a Motel 6 for the call girl to show.

Cost you double, she said.

It's a *doll*, I said. See?

What's his name?

The call girl undressed.

Howdy Doody.

Pyromaniac is not enough, my inner child said. Nor armed robber. Whoremonger neither. Bigger titles await me.

Like what?

Commander in Chief. He fingered his nose ring.

Give it up.

Next best, then.

First Lady?

Presidential assassin.

Forty-seven motorcycle police accompanied the motorcade as it sailed down the interstate. The motorcade itself consisted of six stretch limousines with black windows.

Which one do we shoot?

How the hell do I know?

It's possible that none of them are motoring the Head of State anywhere. Decoys.

We were hiding in the bushes above a drainage ditch alongside the highway.

Can't we start with a lesser figure, like a senator, or a mayor?

Let's blow up some judges.

Are you *crazy*?

We blew up a judge's aluminum tool shed—he was playing scratch golf, his wife, a court stenographer, was in court, his children were adults, his dogs were in the doghouse—with a homemade bomb constructed out of household materials from a design my inner child and I found in a homemade bomb manual. We were at the Texas Gun and Knife Show, standing at a table of AK-47's, Colt Sporters, and .44 Scorpions.

Look, my inner child said, pointing to a rack of khaki colored manuals. *How to Booby Trap a Sofa. Bombs from Golf Balls.* The dealer behind the table on a stool sat chewing a toothpick. He looked at my inner child and hooked a thumb in his Lone Star belt. I'll be goddamned, he said.

A Mason, my inner child said, obviously not in touch with his feelings.

He picked up a handbook and read. *Hit Man: How to Become an Independent Contractor.*

Should we get it, just in case?

In case of what?

The bomb blew out the windows of the house. The dogs howled. The tool shed (and the house) burned to the ground, we read in *The Dallas Morning News*, and the judge (and the SPCA) offered a five thousand dollar reward for information leading to the apprehension and conviction of the parties responsible. We were riding first class on a Southwest flight to Las Vegas. The stewardess brought us round after round.

Pity about them dogs.

We checked into Glitter Gulch, where we gambled, drank, whored, and played golf. I felt like a citizen restored to a birthright. I refused to burn down a single building, or set fire to a car, house, garage, or barn, despite the promptings of my inner child. I turned over a new leaf, I thought. Several. I was tempted to rake them into a pile and light them, but the city had rules. It hardly mattered. We were arrested two days later.

You used the judge's *credit* cards.

He had no use for them, my inner child said.

Put that freaking doll away!

I want to see my lawyer, my inner child said.

I *am* your goddamned lawyer, my lawyer shouted, and realizing he had addressed my inner child *as a person*, slammed his fist down on the metal table. A guard looked through the window on the door.

They've got witnesses at the gunshow, eyewitnesses and videotape from the bank and convenience store, chemicals found in the trunk of the rental car, the arson investigator's report linking those chemicals with the golf balls and the manual with the judge's house, *and* stolen credit cards. Not to mention a possible connection to the armed robbery of a Loomis armored car. Wearing Nixon masks. What a cliché!

You said it was Brink's, I said to my inner child.

And motive, he shouted again. The judge whose house you bombed sent you up for ten years for *arson*.

A coincidence, I said.

How am I supposed to enter a plea of innocent?

Can I bum a light? my inner child asked.

I stood before the judge. He was joking with the district attorney about his golf game.

You play golf? I asked. He ignored me. Pa played golf. All the time. Whupped me with his sand wedge if I didn't clean his clubs good.

The judge pointed his gavel. You're a hair's breadth from contempt.

Pa, my inner child said, Oh Pa oh Pa don't whup me with a sand wedge. Use a driver please. It don hurt so bad.

Bailiff, take that blasted doll. The D.A. laughed, and then the rest of the court laughed, confident now it was allowed to. Yesterday my lawyer had petitioned the court, arguing (only after I threatened to report his unprofessional attitude concerning my *inner child* to the Texas State Bar, The American Psychological Association, Amnesty International, etc.) that it was imperative the doll be allowed to appear with the defendant unfettered during the lengthy proceedings, citing the considerable therapy the accused had already undergone before and during his initial incarceration, but the D.A. responded by suggesting that the therapy had in fact done little if any good, but merely gave an eighth grade drop out an excuse for setting more fires, and furthermore for not only burning down but bombing houses *in addition to* committing aggravated armed robbery. But the judge too was enjoying the moment.

Contempt, he said to my inner child. He was trying not to laugh. Now get that damn doll out of here, he said to the bailiff.

The bailiff and I had a tug-of-war over my inner child. Ahh Jesus, my inner child cried, Ahh Jesus. In the struggle the bailiff ripped off one of my inner child's arms. The event brought back a memory of long ago. I too had once had an arm torn off—broken, truth be told—by an abusive uncle, an ex-marine who sold tractors in the Panhandle, when drunk he swung me around and around for laughs at a Lodge meeting in Amarillo. The broken limb healed with only a minor crook in the forearm (Ma set it with fence picket and feedsack), but my family secret needed clarifying: what did having an arm broken by a drunk uncle have to do with my irresistible urge to burn down buildings? I saw the road to recovery before me, it was long and lonesome, it wasn't much of a road, either, more like a trail, or a rut, with hazards alongside, and houses every which way whispering *Burn me*, but at least I was on the way to recovery, perhaps the rut to recovery would one day lead to the road, and then the interstate, and then the turnpike, but wouldn't I have to rob and burn down another house to have money for the toll? It was a very sad rut to look at. I decided I wasn't sick, so why should I have to walk that damn road anyway?

I'll see *you* in court, my inner child said to the bailiff, who tore his head off.

Televangelist at the Texas Motel

Pestilence and blood, stiffnecked pride! The daughters of Zion are haughty and walk with outstretched necks and wanton eyes, walking and mincing as they go, making a tinkling with their feet, scarlet with sin, clad with lust and tongued as vipers. Therefore will the Lord discover their secret parts.

May the Lord give you scabs upon your head, and take away the bravery of your noisy feet, the chains from your ankles and bracelets from your hands, the bonnets and headbands, the earrings and nose jewels, the changeable suits of apparel and the mantle, the wimples and crisping pins, the glasses and fine linen, the crotchless panties and g-strings, may the Lord discover your secret parts.

And it shall come to pass, that instead of sweet smell there shall be stink; instead of a girdle a rent; instead of well-set hair baldness; instead of a stomacher a girdling sackcloth; instead of damask cheeks boils on your painted face; burning instead of beauty. On your knees, daughter of Zion, whore of Babylon, dogs shall eat the flesh of Jezebels and their carcasses shall be as dung upon the face of the earth. Pray for the redemption of your sin, the whoreseed of sand and the offspring of thy bowels like gravel, from a multitude of sorceries. Shake it! Then shall ye suck, and be satisfied. I will choose your delusions, and visit fears like locusts upon your face, for you do evil before *mine* eyes, and choose that in which I delight O God, *O God*, O gosh, who in Judah hath felt such things? Seething bones! Deep ditches of whoredom! What hast thou seen in Moab? Aholah, lewdness and neighing, hogjaws and butterbags, damnation on your hams! The sweetmeats of heaven are not for the wicked, your mouth is full of dust and the stench of your flesh rises to the nostrils of heaven. Bend over. The eye of God accuses, for you have loosened the loins of a king, and given the treasures of darkness and the riches of abominable places. High tide of Hell! Sweet flames of damnation! Suffering succotash! Goddamn the wicked in their noisy places, ashtrays of filth and velvet paintings of beaches. Bedspreads of sin. Motel matches.

Slave for a Day

My name was N. Boy John. The project was part of the Federal Reparations Act of 20__. I was assigned a family and given an address.

I drove to Lithonia, the City of Granite, ten miles south of Stone Mountain and Sherman's first stop after sacking Atlanta, where the United Daughters of the Confederacy conceived a bas-relief of Jefferson Davis, General Lee, and Stonewall Jackson on the north face of the pluton that took six decades to complete, and where the second Klan was hatched, the Knights of Mary Phagan in attendance, the solemn oath administered in the light of a burning cross by Nathan Bedford Forrest II. So the second page of the form read. Legend has it Sherman, the form did not say, torched Lithonia's railroad station but spared the Lodge when he saw out front a Masonic apron and its all-seeing eye draped over a rocking chair.

Directions took me into Sandstone Estates, a subdivision of million-dollar mansions built in the early 1990s. Through the unwritten rule of OKOP—Our Kind of People—it was exclusively Afro-Saxon.

I parked my truck on the street and looked for signs of life. It was Wednesday afternoon. The moment a head of household signed the forms, my hours began.

I sat in the truck. Nothing. The house, a sandstone pink, was three stories high, as wide as a cargo ship, with a five car garage attached. The long drive circled a fountain. Thin white columns rose to Doric capitals, which held aloft a pedimented gable and a frieze depicting the African diaspora.

The family, the _____, had two children, nine and thirteen. The master was a Vice President of Sun Trust Bank and the mistress a food architect for Griffith Laboratories headquartered in Lithonia (Buffalo Wings Technovations, Traditional and Ethnic Wing Profiles, etc).

A woman in a maid's outfit looked at me from a second story window and disappeared. I rang the bell. It rang slow and sonorous, as if announcing the arrival of an ambassador. The door opened an inch.

Yes, she said.

I'm the _____'s bondsman.

Around the rear, she said.

In the back was an Olympic-size swimming pool

Wax the floor, she said.

Which floor.

There. She pointed to a building.

Machine, instruction inside. She put down a pitcher of ice water. If you thirsty.

Can you sign these forms?

No.

I can't start until forms are signed.

Wax the floor. There. She went inside and closed the door. A bolt shot home.

In the building was a full-sized basketball court, with glass backboards, and three-row bleachers. The waxing machine sat in the corner with a note attached. It was pages long.

I went out behind the building. There was a small muddy man-made lake. I smoked a joint and skipped rocks.

What's your name.

I turned around. A girl with short pink-bowed pigtails stood staring.

N***** Boy John.

Pleased to meet you. My name is Abigail. Abby for short.

We shook hands.

Delidia said you were waxing the floor.

I can't start until your parents sign this form.

My mother will be home in an hour. Then I have riding lessons.

What should I do.

Play basketball, she asked.

Naa.

I don't like basketball either. Come with me.

We went through the kitchen and dining room to the foyer. Fourteen-foot ceilings, chandeliers. The sculpture of a naked man falling to his knees, his hands and feet chained, his back crisscrossed with iron scars, sat at the foot of the stairs.

We went up the winding staircase.

No, No, No, Delidia said. He is not allowed in the house.

It's okay, Abby said. He's going to help me finish a puzzle.

In her room queen-sized bunk beds, stuffed animals, movie posters. A rocking horse, a bozo punching bag, a thousand dolls piled on shelves.

She opened her walk-in closet.

You may enter.

In the corner on the floor sat what looked like a dollhouse covered with a sheet. Like a magician she whisked it off.

What do you think?

From the limb of a papier-mâché tree a naked Barbie doll was hanged. Her blonde hair was brushed to perfection.

What do you think?

Abby, come down here this instant.

At the foot of the stairs stood her mother.

Mommy, this is N***** Boy John.

I held out my hand. It floated there.

Don't *use* that word in this house, Abby's mother said. Get ready. We're leaving in five minutes. To me she said, Papers.

I gave her the forms. She signed them.

It's 4:00. The contract expires in exactly 24 hours. Wax the basketball court. When you're done, Delidia will give you dinner. There's a cot in the gym. Tomorrow morning Delidia will have a list of chores.

Are you the one who invented the Cajun Spicy wing mix?

Do not speak unless spoken to, do you hear. Do you hear? I said, *do you hear*.

In the gym I read the instructions. I stepped out back and smoked another joint. The instructions were no less confusing. First, the floor needed to be finished, not waxed. But first it needed to be cleaned. Then finished and buffed. The machine was not a waxing machine but an electric burnisher.

I knocked on the kitchen door that let out on the patio in front of the pool.

You want me to burnish the floor? I asked.

She closed the door and locked it.

With the machine I buffed the floor for two hours and gave it a very wet look. I was starved.

At the kitchen door Delidia handed me a plate of food. Two McDonald's cheeseburgers.

That's it? She shut the door. What are they having? I went around the side of the house and looked in the dining room window. The father sat carving a roast. Abby kicked her brother under the table. Delidia served the vegetables. She saw me. *Go away.*

I ate the hamburgers and unfolded the cot and lay down with a blanket and a pillow.

I woke up to the gym lights. Abby's brother and three friends ran down the court taking shots.

Who's he, one asked Abby's brother. Abby's brother explained.

No shit. I heard about that.

You'll get one soon. In alphabetical order.

Yo, nigga, another said, come here and tie my shoes.

I lay back down.

You heard him. Tie his shoes.

Fuck you.

The first basketball hit me in the side, the next in the head. I lost count. I picked up the cot and used it as a shield.

You done.

Tie my shoes.

All right already, I said.

Cool, he said. They passed the ball around, ignoring me, while I tied his shoes together.

Satisfied.

Don't back-talk me.

He tripped and fell hard on the floor, hitting his elbow. He groaned, rolling on the glowing hardwood floor, *Jesus Christ*, my funny bone. His friends laughed.

I think it's broken, he said.

Get up, you wuss, Abby's brother said.

They got tired of me and played basketball for an hour. I sat by the lake until they left.

I went to my truck and fetched a bottle of whiskey. I drank half of it before I passed out.

It was still dark when the gym door opened. Three men in sweats wheeled in a wooden whipping post.

Get up boy. I recognized Abby's father.

Another threw me a Kevlar vest.

Time for a whipping.

Why, what did I do?

You don't have to do nothing, boy. We never did nothing but we were whipped.

I didn't whip you.

No, you didn't. But your cracker bastard ancestors whipped mine.

Your ancestors were cracker bastards?

Hell no they weren't no cracker bastards.

Neither were mine.

I put on the jacket. They tied me to the whipping post. For twenty minutes, at first methodically, then with increasing intensity, and finally with a mad abandon and frenzy of blood lust, they whipped me on the back, occasionally missing the jacket, which drew blood and cries.

Shut up wigger, shut the fuck up you goddamn wigger.

Spent, they untied me.

Clean up the mess, Abby's father said. Delidia will give you first-aid. He turned to his neighbors.

We still going for a run? he asked. It's five-fifteen. Let's hit it.

I drank whiskey and smoked a joint in the gym. Delidia brought me a bowl of cornflakes.

The list of chores was a mile long. Clear the cobwebs out of the rafters of the gym. Clean the mortar between the bricks of the patio with a toothbrush. Dig a six foot hole and fill it with bricks. Wax the skis, polish the sailboat brass, prune the bonsai with surgical scissors.

At noon Delidia brought me lunch, a bowl of rancid beans and moldy bread. I washed it down with whiskey and smoked half a joint and mowed the back lawn with a rusty push mower, despite the tantalizing 100 Series John Deere—on which a handwritten note was taped, *Do Not Touch*—sitting in the garage next to mountain bikes, jet skis, and a dozen lacrosse sticks.

At 2:30 Abby and a friend came to the pool where I was scrubbing the diving board with Clorox.

Out of my face, punkass chump, Abby's friend said. She did a perfect swan dive. They splashed around and then went inside and watched cartoons.

At three-thirty the mistress pulled round the drive and honked. Abby and her friend jumped into the convertible.

You, she said to me.

Me? I asked.

Yes, you. You have thirty minutes left. Rake the drive. She sped off. Her tires spat gravel.

I lay down on the cot in the gym and feel asleep. Someone kicked the cot.

Wake up. You're done.

It was Abby's father.

But the chores. The hole in the ground, the bricks.

You're serious.

I'm not leaving.

What do you mean, you're not leaving.

I'm not leaving.

Suit yourself.

Delidia asked me what I wanted for dinner. Roast beef, scalloped potatoes, a salad, iced tea.

You have led a good life, no.

Not particularly, why?

No reason.

In the morning I was stripped down to my underwear and tied to a tree in the yard. The three men broke out brand new diamondback steerhide whips.

What about the Kevlar.

What about it, Abby's father said.

In a matter of minutes I passed out. I woke up on my stomach on the cot. Delidia dressed the wounds.

Not so bad, she said. A few scars. You leave now?

I'm not leaving.

Abby's brother and his friends brought me a coke.

I thought it was only for a day, a friend said to Abby's brother.

Guess not.

You need anything.

Marijuana.

An hour later they came back with a dank spongy ounce and rolled a joint. We sat by the lake in the dark and smoked it.

Where you from, Abby's brother asked.

California.

For real.

I was born in Gothenburg.

Where's that.

Sweden.

No shit.

Abby's father shouted from an upstairs window. One of the friends dinched the joint and took off running. The brother went in the opposite direction.

You seen my son?

The father stood right behind me.

No. I waited for him to kick me.

You staying.

I'm not leaving.

Rest up, boy. Saturday we're going to the *country*.

I slept off and on all day Friday. The scabs on the wounds cracked and bleed. I gave Delidia fifty dollars and asked her to buy me a bottle of whiskey. She looked at me. I gave her another twenty.

The next morning a truck with six bloodhounds in the camper pulled up. The three men threw me in the back with the dogs, which barked and howled and nipped and snapped. Thirty minutes later we pulled down a rutted dirt drive to a hunting cabin. Abby's father dropped the tailgate and the dogs, their nails ticking, scrambled off the truck bed.

Get out, he said.

I'm not leaving.

They pulled me by the legs.

Run, a neighbor said.

Where.

Wherever you like.

I took off. Five minutes later I heard a shotgun blast. The dogs barked and bayed closer and closer.

I broke through underbrush and fell into a ditch. I climbed up onto a paved road. A flatbed approached carrying a generator. I waved it down.

They're going to kill me, I said. Help me.

The two men shook their heads and drove on.

I climbed a live oak. One by one the dogs found the tree. They leapt and leapt. The three men showed up.

Who gets the first shot, Abby's father said.

They drew pine needles.

They shot at me and missed. One pellet struck my anklebone. Another struck my side.

Is he dead yet, a neighbor asked.

Hell no, the other said. He ain't ready for dead yet. He ain't *earned* dead yet.

We camped in the woods. In the middle of the night I woke up to a bright light. A cross was burning. Three men in sheets chanted mumbo jumbo about ghouls and dragons and one-eyed giants.

They tied my hands behind my back and doused me with water from a gasoline can and hoisted me thirty feet in the air by a rope thrown over a tree branch.

You'll never look at our women again, Abby's father said. You see one coming you cross the street. You hear?

I'm not leaving.

Torch the bastard, a neighbor said.

Light him up, the other said.

They took me down and threw me in the cabin shower.

Wash up. You smell like a landfill.

Around a fire they gave me whiskey.

I took a joint out of a baggie in my shoe and lit it. One neighbor, then the other, then Abby's father, toked and passed it along.

Game's up, the father said. We've had our fun.

I'm not leaving.

Goddamn crazy motherfucker. What next, he asked his neighbor.

They talked it over. I made a few suggestions.

The next day they chained a mattress to the truck and dragged me around the neighborhood, drinking whiskey from a jug and firing shotguns in the air.

A cop pulled up.

What the hell.

Abby's father explained.

You okay with this? the cop asked.

I'm not leaving.

For weeks I was beaten, shot at, cursed, kicked, slapped, thumped, whipped, and punched.

One day they wrapped me in heavy gauge chain and threw me in the pool. That was it. I'd had enough.

No drowning, I said. Set me on fire. But no water.

The man don't like water, Abby's friend said to his neighbor. Go figure. The son of a bitch don't like water.

It's not the water, I said, it's the chains.

You ain't leaving yet.

My day is up. I've got to get back.

Back to what.

He had a point.

Late at night Abby sometimes brought me cookies and milk. The son kept me knee deep in dope, Delidia discovered she liked whiskey as much as I did. One morning I woke up to find her naked beside me.

Delidia.

Sí.

Run away with me.

We planned our escape. It was an elaborate hoax, not the first, not the last, but it worked nevertheless.

In Mexico City we pawned the mistress's jewelry. The forged cashier's check from Coca Cola landed safely in the numbered account. The Scandinavian Airlines airbus lifted from the Aeropuerto Internacional Benito Juárez runway and flew us northeast to Stockholm. Halfway there we discovered the pellet wound in my side was infected. I burned with high fever for six hours and fell asleep watching a movie about miserable American lovers in London who loathed themselves and each other. The hatchet-faced actress had teeth a horse would envy.

In Stockholm, we went straight to the nearest primary care center. Children in the waiting room stared at Delidia. We waited and waited and waited.

The doctor numbed my side and dug and plucked the pellet out with tweezers.

What have we here, he said.

I explained the Federal Reparations Act.

He looked at me as if I had gone mad. He wrote a prescription for antibiotics. In Sweden, he said, we feel guilty about everything all the time. Why be so specific?

I couldn't give him an answer. I told him I was born in Gothenburg, so I understood the guilt part. The rest was America.

Delidia and I checked into The Grand Hotel quayside on Södra Blasieholmshamnen across the water from the Royal Palace. Below us replicas of the Gokstad and dragon-headed longships tied to the dock floated with their sails down and oars drawn up. We took a bath and ordered up a bottle of Jack Daniels and lay on the bed watching the snow drift in the twilight.

Deadly

The other day I woke up dead. What next? I'd quit my job at the chicken plant and my wife, who is the heaviest abstainer in Texas, left me this time, she said, waving a vacuum wand in my face, *for good*. It was true. She'd been gone for a month, during which time I drank gallons of tequila, vodka, rum, scotch, ale, stout, wine, beer, grain, and one scrumptious bottle of 'Lectric Shave, which shore me like a sheep.

The last thing I remember before waking up dead was stopping at a convenience store for a 12-pack. It was nine a.m. I was on foot, too civic-minded to drive. Truth to tell, my wife had raced my pick-up to San Antonio, since she is perpetually in a race, God knows where, and moved in with her sister, a tax lawyer and an angry appendage of the IRS, which entitles her to carry firearms. My wife called to tell me she was slapping me with a lawsuit for mental cruelty. Sister-in-law got on the line and reassured her the feds sanctioned threats against lowlifes with her government-issue snub nose if lowlifes couldn't get their shit in one accountable pile. Sell the house and send the money. We are a dysfunctional family unit, my wife said, praise Jesus. He's a *drunk*, in-law said.

Whose family did she mean? Sister-in-law put her .38 to the phone. I heard the cylinder go clickety-click.

I wasn't afraid of guns when I woke up. Fact is, I was spoiling for a fight. Let that bag-ass point a gun at me now! I'll rip off my arm and throw it at her. *Ha.*

I guess one night I blacked out. For good.

Rigor mortis underdescribes. I felt stiff as a poker. Joints whining, I eased myself out of the hole in the floor where I found myself half stuck. A crowbar and floorboards studded with rusty nails lay beside the hole. I've done some dumb shit drunk but ripping up the floor beats all. My bones ached. My skin felt like a roadside shoe. I determined how long I'd been gone. Eleven days, judging from liquor receipts. I examined myself in the closet door's full-length mirror.

Hungover I wasn't, though. I felt oddly elated, if confused. I left my bedroom, which had been stripped of furniture and of all domestic comforts, even the 40"

Hitachi I won in a national Publishers Clearing House sweepstakes three years ago, my single stroke of good fortune in twenty-eight years of meaningless suffering numbed, of course, with at least fourteen annums of delicious drinking. What the deuce.

I went down the hall. Turning the corner to the kitchen, I ran headlong into my wife, who was carrying an Absolut box of barbecue utensils. I recognized the meat saw my uncle had given me on graduation day.

Martha, I said.

She screamed. No respect whatsoever for the dead

I chased her out of the house and down the drive. A black Mercedes peeled off from the curb. My wife climbed into her Accord and locked the doors. Always in a hurry! And where was my truck? Martha was shaking, crying so violently she couldn't get the keys into the ignition. The engine wouldn't start. What luck! I was on a roll, happy as an idiot, given my condition. I danced around the car, hocking maggots on the windshield, saying I had come from the dead to roast her over an open pit with plantains. She kept screaming, *I'm sorry, I'm sorry*, which confused me, since I was tormenting *her* now.

The engine revved, Martha raced backwards down the drive, knocking over our mailbox, and laid smoking rubber down the block. Always in a hurry.

Good riddance. The cowboy lawyer she was entertaining nightly in San Antone would never look the same.

I went to the kitchen and buttered my joints, easing the hinge wheeze, the worst part, I decided, about being a dud. I sprayed myself with liquid plastic from an aerosol can, which prevented any more of me from falling off than was absolutely necessary, except to scare the next living ninny.

I am—*was*—a college-educated redneck. Not bad for the son of sodbusters. First in my family to get a college degree. Goddamn good it did. I met Martha, of course, in a bar, back when she partook. I graduated from Texas A & M with a degree in poultry engineering. I dreamed one day of having my own brand, with classy advertisements of rainwet women endowed with plump and tender chicken parts, myself as company mascot, decked out in a chicken costume my wife, an interior decorator for a double-wide trailer manufactory, agreed to design. My first job was with Big Chicken, a Texas trademark. I started out in processing. I shoveled manure atop a Depression Yazoo. I decided early on a man ought not to begin his career shoveling chicken shit, but

Martha and I jacked seventeen credit cards to the limit, with cash advances to pay off cash advances, late fee on top of late fee, at 29.99 percent—paying minimum payments I'd have to live 30,000 years—so I found neither the time nor the capital to build my first coop. I shoveled weekends, holidays. My life dream was swallowed up in clouds of ammonia. I drank heavily, with less and less pleasure. In college I played baseball. I was the best bunter in the history of the conference. Check the records. After seven years of head-on drinking my gut swoll up. Face too. A blowfish of ethanol. Wife said No to sex. Big banana. One day she badgered me about drug dependency and lowered self-esteem. Bigger banana still. She recommended an exercise program, *Jumping for Joy*. I declined and opened a liter of vodka. She said I needed counseling, and recommended a clinic. She was tired of being a codependent. Who could blame her, if that's what she was?

I complained about my fatal employ.

I want a *chicken*. I was too tired to say *empire*.

Patience, she said. I was home for lunch. It was a hundred and ten degrees outside. She jogged around the living room in sweat pants, with the window unit going great guns. Her sweatshirt said, Power.

It took Colonel Sanders twenty years, she said, shaking the sweat from her hair, to build his empire. *Cosmopolitan* just voted him one of the sexiest men of the century.

Was she joking? She must have had a thing for the Colonel. I took two tugs off the bottle and put it back in the freezer. I opened a can of beer and stood in the doorway. Martha stopped exercising and cut a look just to the side of my tire, afraid it might bounce her off the wall.

It's never too late, she said, to start working out.

When I woke up a corpse, I saw her point.

I went to the tool room and secured my head to my torso with a staplegun. For shits and grins I sawed two dowels off a broom. With Crazy Glue I stuck them to my temples.

I phoned The President and First Lady Health and Fitness Club for a personalized self-improvement session. I told the receptionist I was in lousy shape and wanted to change my life. A hard body is a *hard body*, she said. Are you aware of your body?

Never more.

What are your goals?

Ripped to the bone.

Sounds definitely fine. Do some warm-ups. We are a conscious organization, so dress to look. Then *feel* it.

She laughed. I laughed too. Coughing, I swallowed a tooth.

Do you smoke?

Lately.

Stop.

She hung up.

I put on a pair of Wells Lamonts and drove to the gym.

I put my face to the tinted window and saw guys in body tights jumping up and down and staring at their well-grazed hides in floor-length mirrors. The gorgeous instructress glimpsed my decomposing face pressed to the pane of the exclusive club. She fainted clean away.

The gym emptied itself of screaming exercisers. I tried to shake their hands, to 'gratulate them on flinty pecs and granite buttocks, but they ran like scalded dogs. Narcissistic sissies! Like they'll live forever!

Sadly, I realized no one would ever want to touch me again. A former college sports star, I scored easy. My Aggie girlfriend let me bury my face in her breasts, where I dreamt of genetically engineered six-foot chickens on steroids, thighs like a pro halfback's, sure to fetch the blue-ribbon ten grand at the Livestock Show and Rodeo, Houston, Texas. Now love seemed hopeless, until I found another walking dead. A zaftig girl, one whose flesh might remain on the bone for weeks, tenderized by microorganisms. No model giraffes for me! Zaftig and I would agree to close our eyes.

The gym deserted, I worked out. I lost a forearm on the decline press. I needed a drink.

The man at the liquor store where I usually bought my bottles looked through the bulletproof glass.

You *rough*, he said.

I purchased a quart of Absolut and downed it on the spot.

I bummed a smoke from a passing drunk, but lit the methane consequent of body rot. I staggered onto the street. Blue flame hissed from the cracks in my skin. Pedestrians and passers-by caused a chain-reaction of fender-benders. I rolled in the roadside gravel and put myself out. Thank God my nose, what was left of it, couldn't smell a thing.

On the sidewalk a young man wearing gigantic jeans and a Giants jersey, with hair greased forward like a '50s dashboard, stepped up beside me and gazed round and round. At first I thought he was one of the living dead who *was* really dead, and not just kidding himself. Frankenstein, he said, where are the *cameras*?

A shotgun blast took off my left leg. A squad car had pulled over, lights whirring. Surrender.

Surrender what?

Put your hands on top of your head.

This is a movie set, I said. I made a sweeping gesture with my missing forearm. The officer stood up and took off his mirrored sunglasses, looking around for cameras.

Don't move, I said.

I hopped backwards on my remaining peg and blocked the way of a maroon Seville. With my hideous choppers I pulled an old man from behind the wheel.

See you soon, he said. He chewed his gums, and called me governor.

I drove to the outskirts of town and headed north through the Blue Mountains to San Saba, not far from the Colorado River, the dead-center Texas town I am heir to, as my birthright entitles me to bear the family coat of arms, an ordinary of plowhorses.

Along the way I stopped at a 7-Eleven and picked up a suitcase of beer, which the clerk gave me free of charge, if only I would wake him up, he said, since he had worked a double shift, and was only dreaming. Still, he kept laughing. Maybe he was used to dead folk, given the shacks down the road.

I bought some Bazooka, and, chewing, thumbed through the latest issue of *Longevity*. What a sack of shit. Advertisements for vitamins, ginseng, organic wrinkle cream. An article on immortality.

I flung my jawbone like a horseshoe to the rack of skin rags behind the counter. A dead ringer. The clerk fell over.

I retrieved my chops and rehinged them. On the way out I bumped into a drunk black dude.

My man, he said.

Dead man, I said.

I hear. He was carrying a Glad bag of empties. He high-fived the air. You Willie's son? he asked.

Same.

I thought you joined the *Army*, man.

I did.

You on sick leave?

Colitis. Nothing much.

You *a*wol? Not *Willie* son. You got any change?

I handed him a beer, and a five spot.

Looking good. Looking good. You tell Willie Fred's gonna *smoke* his ass if he don't lay off the Diesel. *Man* five big ones thank you *sir*. What was your name?

Theodore.

God loves you, Theodore. Now run on home and take a bath, boy. You stink.

Down the road I drove-thru Popeye's for some Cajun wings. The cashier, a high school type with a braid of orange hair, tossed the box of chicken wings through the window. She hugged herself and shrieked. My skull sutures ground back and forth and cracked open like mouths of broken teeth.

Chill out, I said.

She was wearing earbuds. She hadn't even noticed me!

She disappeared to the fryer, which was smoking. She brought up the basket. The strings of potato looked like burnt worms.

Fries, I said.

She ignored me.

But I *am* worm, I said. I drew a long one out of my nose. See?

She danced around in circles.

Your mother's a worm! I said. So is your sister! A tooth flew out of my mouth. It ricocheted off the register. I tore off my foot, which was beginning to offend me, and tossed it through the window. I plucked out an eye.

If worms don't die, we burn in hell! She ignored me still.

Over the register was a calendar. A greased body builder in bikini briefs pumped hundred-pound dumbbells. He looked like my genetically engineered chicken, only plucked. I've had some dumbshit ideas but a six-foot chicken beats all. Anyhow, there was enough rot on that carcass to fertilize an acre of feed.

I parked.

I picked up a bird wing with my teeth and looked in the rear view mirror. There was a hole in my forehead.

The wing looked so helpless. I wondered about the bird's relatives, and if it had a sister, and which had died first, and if it were ever aware it was serving a death sentence at a poultry farm, which I decided it didn't, otherwise no one could eat chickens with a clear conscience, and, anyhow, aware of death, it would have figured out how to fly, and escaped. I started crying. I couldn't stop. I tried the complimentary coleslaw. No wonder they gave it away. I spat it out the window. A woman on her way into the restaurant hustled her five kids through the door. Maybe she thought I was a sex killer, or a television reporter.

I threw the car into reverse and stomped the accelerator, running over a trashcan of chicken boxes, where a street bum was rummaging for supper.

Lord have mercy, he said, why are you crying?

I'm from the Health Department. This place is condemned.

Good sir, the scavenger said, perhaps a man of your understanding can see I am in desperate need of a nourishing meal. Do you know of a charitable mission close by where I might find refreshment?

Eat some worms, I said, and levitate. I tossed him a twenty.

He hopped in. I used to sell insurance, he said.

And?

Everybody dies. I didn't have the heart to say differently. At every opportunity I told my clients, Soon you die. What about insurance? they'd ask. What's the point? I was not popular. I was terminated, thank God. One night under a clear autumn sky I wandered out of my house. I forgot my name, but I felt splendid. He lit a cigar. Do you have a name?

Nope.

A pleasure to make your acquaintance. My name is Happy.

Down the road we devised a plan. He bought an ice chest, two cases of beer, and a can of Zippo.

Our first stop was The Commonwealth Bank in Marble Falls. I hobbled into the lobby and set myself on fire, while Happy instructed the stricken tellers to fill a grocery bag with cash. We hit eleven small-town banks in two days. I was as black as a barbecue pit. I was falling apart.

Home, I said. He handed me a beer.

I understand.

We drank.

A band of angels, he said.

A passel of worms.

I am a man of faith.

Shoot a lawyer.

What kind?

Have you ever been murdered by a sister-in-law?

I was twice divorced.

Do I smell?

A smidgen.

He directed me to an overpass that crossed a wide creek. Bums stood around a barrel fire. One reclined in a battered La-Z-Boy, smoking a cigar. Others bathed in the creek. Relatives? I asked.

By circumstance, good sir. Thanks for the lift.

Anytime.

He lit a cigar with a fifty.

We'll see you later, he said.

Not much. You look half-dead yourself.

In the by and by.

Wait, I said. He was passing out twenties. He was saying, Shit tickets.

Yes? he asked.

On Judgment Day, will I look like this?

Oh yes. At first.

Then what?

He laughed, and waved me off.

I drove to my uncle's farm south of San Saba and ditched the car in the woods. Not much of me left. Half an arm, a leg, a collapsing torso. The gas leaks have stopped. I sleep under an abandoned wheelbarrow, watching the days go by, one blending pleasantly enough into the next, with occasional drizzles of rain. I'm waiting for a band of angels. Failing that, I want nothing more than to pass out for good. Waking up dead ain't no hair of the dog.

Ginny Shay

He followed her to Island Grove. She spread out a blanket and sat with friends and waited for the music to begin. The Third Annual Blues Fest. Party Till the Cows Come Home.

She took off her shirt, beneath which she wore a pale blue two-piece bathing suit, and rubbed suntan lotion on her legs and chest and neck. One by one the group of five girls rubbed lotion onto one another's backs and sprayed themselves head to toe against the black flies.

Lambs preparing themselves for their own slaughter! Most pitiful, most terrible. Seasoning their shanks and loins for the hellish spits, where The Sustainer of Worlds will roast them to sesame gold. Most Benevolent, most Merciful, may the flames of the pit lick their lascivious legs writhing to the dithyrambs, the pagan frenzies Your Prophet slew with his bright sword!

He sat under the shade of a tree smoking, watching. Her name was Ginny Shay. Ms. Shay, the professor called her. They sat in the same graduate education class. He could not take his eyes off the whiteness of her neck, the whiteness of her arms, the milky whiteness of the cleavage she revealed with no more self-consciousness than a bat in the natural history museum in Denver hanging upside down in the dark. The whiteness of her hands, the blondness of her hair, the blueness of her eyes. So horrible against the perfect leavening, the perfect bread baked to a perfect brown, as terrible as the bread left in the oven too long, burned a monstrous black. Between these two extremes there was a new destiny. Not the dark amusements of descendants of chattel, their teeth in pink mouths laughing against the smoky onyx of their hides, their depraved idleness, their love of music and dancing and fornication. Not the pale depravities of the new barbarians, their women enslaved by illusions of freedom, wallowing in the sties of lust and greed, driven by drums played by their primitive counterparts to descend into the thick mire, nor the flesh of leg and breast and back, their faces painted like harlots', their nauseating perfumes, their eyelashes crusted with tar, lips swollen open and red as blood, open and willing and waiting.

Tariq, a voice said. He looked up. The music had stopped. Ginny stood a few feet away in sandals wearing a button down shirt with tails that fell mid-thigh.

Ginny, he said.

You want to join us?

I'm waiting for a friend.

When she shows up, come join us. We're right over there.

Thank you.

How do you like the music.

Okay. And you.

Hands trembling, he lit another cigarette.

Great. You want a beer?

What do you think of the seminar? he asked.

Dr. Dworkin's? I'm here to get certified, if I don't die of boredom first.

Yes. Certified.

Why are you here.

Similar. The same.

You have a job back home?

I want to teach in the States. And you?

I'm going back to Denver.

Denver. What's in Denver.

Shepherd of the Hills. My old job.

You were let go?

You have to be certified now to teach in private school. I haven't learned a thing in two semesters.

Me either. What do you teach?

Math. And you.

Chemistry.

Impressive.

The next band started up.

Bye now, Ginny said.

Her long shaved legs carried her across the grass to the group of friends now joined by men. American lawns and their orgies in the grass. Demented animals who believed they were individuals. Utterly blind, without thought or guidance, without submission to the Compassionate, the Merciful. Ginny laughed and covered her mouth. She caught him looking at her and waved him over.

Late Wednesday night he stood in the dark on the sidewalk a half a block from the Queen Anne house where she rented an apartment on the second floor. A pink and blue grotesquerie, with spindles and stickwork and stained glass and turrets, an idol to the worship of industry and the fetish of science, wretched pagan excesses the Merciful, the Compassionate, the All Powerful will wipe away with blasts of wind the towers of vain sand from sea to shining sea. A car pulled up to the curb, doors slammed. Laughter.

On the second floor lights came on. The couple moved into the kitchen, then one by one the lights went out, except for pale light, candles, in her bedroom.

A math teacher at a kufr school! Gum-chomping Christian cow of eternal darkness and damnation! He climbed a tree. They lay on her bed naked and smoking, passing a joint back and forth in the flickering light of fat candles. Dope smoking beer swilling swine. O Most Merciful, with your mighty sword slaughter the pigs as they wallow in filth, writhing to the pounding of pagan drums and the wailing of the damned, clapping and slapping their flesh together like crazed beasts, lost in slavish ecstasy, blind to Your Judgments, Most Merciful! Fear the fire whose fuel is men and stones! Rain-laden clouds! Iblis! Stunning thunder-claps! Our eyes intoxicated, bewitched by sorcery! Painful doom! Terror of death! American riding mowers. One hundred dollar haircuts. Rain from the sky. The heavens your canopy. The earth your couch.

Wind gusts. Cold summer rain slashed through the leaves of the tree where he stood high up on a branch watching her bedroom window. Ginny and her boyfriend appeared at the window, looking at the storm. Lightning lit up the sky, but they did not see him. The neighborhood went dark. Thunder rolled past, rattling windowpanes and setting off car alarms.

The next day she sat across from him at the seminar table.

You never joined us, she said.

I wasn't feeling well. He sneezed and blew his nose.

Did you see that storm last night?

Yes.

We're in the rainshadow of the Rockies.

Rainshadow?

Dr. Dworkin arrived with his beaten leather briefcase, bulbous gut and saddlebags wide as a Jew whore's, though most of the whores he had seen (and paid for) were Iranian exiles. The seminar was long and tedious. The monkey read from his notes. That Dr. Dworkin had not joined his tribe in international finance, banking, internet porn, or arms manufactory made him doubt he was a Jew at all. Perhaps he was a gypsy posing as Jew. A Pakistani acquaintance had told him many American Jews were imposters—gypsies masquerading as Hebrews, interbreeding with the white barbarians of Europe, to climb the social hierarchy of skin tone, where the more one resembled a specter, ghoul, or Casper the Friendly Ghost, the greater one's prospects, regardless of how repulsive the face, pocked with purple acne scars. The professor held forth with sinister niceness. Adolescent psychology. Self-esteem. Decentering the I. Tariq pretended to take notes but drew up an imaginary list of ways in which he would torture Dr. Dworkin. Cut off his hands and feet. Disfigure his face with glowing pokers. Rip out his toenails with needle-nosed pliers. Sever his fingers with a blowtorch. Hang him upside down and saw him in half from his asshole to his jawbone with a dull hacksaw. Bathe him in hydrochloric acid. Skin him alive as efficiently as a Mongolian goat herder skins a Japanese warlord. Ginny asked questions and took notes, pretending to ignore him even as she kicked him under the table twice.

In the library he looked up rainshadow. Storms like the night before were rare in Greeley. It was a judgment on his lust for Ginny.

The next week he sat outside the student union smoking and drinking tea from a Styrofoam cup, imagining the glory to the Compassionate, the Merciful, when every product made from petroleum leeched from the bowels of the earth by demons, in cahoots with his debased and repaganized brothers—its plastic utensils, its roads and dashboards, its CDs and condoms, its computers and cell phones, its lascivious rags exposing every imperfection of flesh, its jellied lumps and stretched teats, its straps of ox muscles and thighs like meat stumps—burst into simultaneous flames in the bright and burning wrath of the Most Merciful's baleful gaze at what the pigs and monkeys had wrought worldwide. A Mighty

Blast. Soon after the Compassionate, the Merciful gave the Believers the gift of fission, then fusion-fission, the skies would rain radioactive blood across the fruited plains, across the mountains east and west, from the sun-scorched deserts of Death Valley to the pestilential towers of New York—the obstinate folly and vanity of skyscrapers!—two of which the Compassionate, the Merciful, had already providentially, stupendously, magnificently, gloriously destroyed, from the whores of Los Angeles to the money-lenders of Wall Street, coast to coast every last American transformed into intergalactic gas and subatomic dust. America's liberty bell will ring hollow, like a skull struck by a stick, or crushed by rocks thrown at an adulteress buried up to her neck in the burning sand.

Feeling better, a voice said.

Ginny stood with a cup of coffee.

Summer colds are the worst, she said. Why is that? Do you mind if I sit?

I'm busy.

Busy what.

Smoking.

Do I look like a body nazi? I don't care if you smoke.

Please, you must leave me alone.

We can't be friends?

I have no friends, he said.

Here?

Anywhere.

Not where you're from? Ginny asked.

No.

Where are you from? she asked.

Where are you from?

Iowa City.

I am Syrian.

Like, Damascus? That's in Syria, right?

Aleppo. My father was a master soap maker.

A friend of mine went to Aleppo and spend days wandering through the shopping bazaar. The one underground, like in Montreal. What's it called?

Souk. It is most certainly not underground.

She's been all over the world. Her dad's a colonel in the army.

Excuse me. He stood up. I must go now and study.

The seminar?

Yes.

What are you doing for your presentation?

You will see.

I wouldn't mind some feedback on mine. My heart's not in it.

Nor mine.

Where my heart doesn't go, my ass goes kicking and screaming. Now I'm curious. What's yours about. Come on. Not even a hint?

I will surprise you.

Okay. She wrote her address and phone number on a slip of paper she tore from a notebook. But call first. My boyfriend won't exactly understand.

Understand what.

We're friends. Right? I've never had a Muslim friend.

What makes you believe I am Muslim.

I just assumed—

I have been profiled before.

I'm sorry. Really, I'm sorry.

In fact, I am a Christian. When I was a boy my family left Syria for Sweden.

Wow. I mean, was it good for your family?

My mother died in childbirth. My father died of a heart attack. I had a choice: go back to Syria or become a ward of the state. I stayed in Sweden. I was adopted by a minister and his wife. Pentecostals. It changed my life. I accepted the Lord into my life when I was thirteen.

She put her hand on his arm. I knew I felt it.

Felt what.

The Holy Spirit.

You are a Christian?

Sometimes. Mostly I'm a sinner. But that's why I'm drawn to you. You seem so pure. Maybe you can help me get back in touch with the Holy Spirit.

I am a sinner too.

Maybe we can pray together. My life's completely out of balance. I'm doing things I thought I'd never do. I've really slipped since I left Sheppard of the Hills. You remember Proverbs. Even in laughter the heart is sorrowful. The end of mirth is heaviness, and the backslider is filled with his own ways.

Saturday afternoon he checked the weather forecast. At midnight he found himself in the tree watching Ginny and her boyfriend.

Taste the fruit of your deeds! Eat of the Sustenance. Contemplate (O Man!) the memorials of the Compassionate, the Merciful! Worm of the Earth, gnawing at his Staff! Ya sin! Lote-trees. Behold! Perish the hands of the Father of Flame! Burnt in the Fire of Blazing Flame! His wife carries the fuel of crackling wood! Ropes of palm-leaf around her neck! Lying forelock! Jizya! Fonts of molten brass! Congealed blood. Scattered fragments. Like ashes quenched and silent. Withered like a date-stalk. Unbelievers, heap them together and cast them into hell.

He spent the next week writing a treatise, the first part of which—beautifully and bluntly entitled *American Beasts and the Undutiful Boy*—he would present to the seminar, connecting it to pedagogy by arguing that Americans, especially white Americans, and in particular white American women, their burning ovens as wide as drinking bowls, are uneducable barbaric sex maniacs, and should therefore be enslaved or buried alive. As for their counterparts, white American men, death was too good for them. The Friday before the presentation he sat at his library carrel, trembling as he wrote.

A girl looks at you, appearing as if she were an enchanting nymph or an escaped mermaid but as she approaches, you sense only the screaming instinct inside her, and you can smell her burning body, not the scent of perfume but flesh, only flesh. Tasty flesh, truly, but flesh nonetheless. O Compassionate, Merciful, guard me against the forward behavior of the American woman, who knows full well the beauties of her body, her face, her exciting eyes, her full lips, her mountainous breasts, her full buttocks and her smooth legs, who wears bright colors that awaken the primitive sexual instincts of the jungle and the cave, hiding nothing, but adding to that the thrilling laugh and the bold look.

Undutiful Boy! Succumbing to the charms of the harlot, the succubus, the dancer and her whorish dance, the voluptuous breasts, the sweet backside shaped like a bell, a harp, a heart begging to be beaten, wrung, clutched, plucked, strummed like a buzuq to the silvery rattle of the daf!

The room convulsed with feverish music. Dancing naked legs filled the hall arms draped around waists, chests met chests, lips met lips, and the atmosphere was full of love and lust and death and blood rained down from the rafters—

Hey you.

He looked up from his desk.

Ginny.

Really working up a sweat.

He put a book in his lap.

You want some coffee? Ginny asked.

No, thank you.

My god, did you hear about the Peeping Tom?

Peeping Tom.

A neighbor saw some guy climbing down from the tree in front of my apartment. Cops found evidence in the leaves.

Evidence.

You know. Wanker. Way up high in a tree. Totally whack. At least they have a DNA sample, in case he turns rapist, which the detective said is like almost always the case. Peeps have exactly the same M.O. Can you believe it?

Yes. I'm afraid I can. Americans are a peculiar breed.

What, you think we're all pervs? You wish. What are you working on?

My presentation.

That night he walked by Ginny's apartment. The blinds were drawn. No doubt Ginny was rutting in the dark with her pale pink ram.

He rang her bell. He rang it again.

A voice came over an intercom.

Go away and go to hell.

Ginny. It's me.

Who is this.

Tariq.

Tariq. What are you doing here?

I need to speak with you.

About what.

My presentation. Our Lord Jesus Christ. The Holy Spirit.

It's a bit late, don't you think? This is like totally embarrassing. I asked you to call first. I'm in no state of mind to pray. Tariq, my heart is black. Black with despair and death and sin.

Ginny, stop crying. I can help change that. Ten minutes. Trust the Lord.

The lock buzzed. He climbed the creaky wooden stairs. The scent of warm soap and shampoo filled the apartment. Artificial perfumes and dyes. An insult to the memory of his father, who at ten through the kindness of an uncle worked as an oven-stoker and ash-pounder and by forty was the among the most esteemed soap makers in Aleppo, before rivals blinded him with lye and doused him with boiling oil. He lived a week, cursing the kafir, the Jew pigs and Christian dogs. Ginny wore a robe and towel around her hair.

Where's your boyfriend.

I don't know. Who cares.

Pardon me?

We broke up.

I'm sorry.

I'm not. One of his frat brothers posted pictures on the internet. From the blues concert.

I remember. Party Till The Cow Comes Home.

Assholes, she said, wiping tears from her eyes. Excuse my French. So tell me about your presentation.

Can I have some ice water.

Sure.

She went into the kitchen. A tray cracked, ice clicked into a glass. He slipped off his belt and wrapped it around his hand. She put a tall glass on the table and sat across from him.

Tell me about your presentation.

He stood up and paced.

It's a comparison of the Islamic and American systems of education. He looked through the blinds. And how the white man, every European and American, is an enemy of Islam. The white man in league with the Zionists has reduced Muslims around the world to self-pity and self-loathing.

Sounds a bit extreme. Is this like the Islamic view?

The doorbell rang over and over again.

Damn it, Ginny said. She went to the intercom.

Who is it.

It's me. Why. You expecting somebody?

Barry, go away.

The web site is down. Permanently. We voted tonight. Mike's out of SAE. Booted. Totally. It wasn't my fault. I didn't know. I swear I didn't know. You know I didn't know.

It's late. We'll talk tomorrow.

Ginny, please, he yelled. I have to see you now. Right now.

Tomorrow.

The Peeping Tom's been spotted.

You lie.

I swear to God.

Then call the cops.

She switched off the speaker.

Barry pounded on the door. *Ginny. Open up. Ginny.* The voice moved into the yard under her bedroom window. *Ginny. Let me in, goddamn it.*

She opened the window. You're drunk. Go home. We'll talk tomorrow.

Shut up everybody, a neighbor shouted, shut up and go to bed.

Ginny closed the window and turning around found herself face to face with Tariq.

My presentation, he said.

He put the belt around her neck.

La ilaha illallahu.

Tariq, Ginny gasped. What—

Her cow eyes swelled from the pressure, a widening abyss of blue and reddening sclera, and went blank.

At four in the morning he let himself out of the apartment. Barry was passed out facedown on the lawn, an empty bottle of Jack Daniels like a stuffed animal tucked under his arm.

At his apartment Tariq took off his clothes and shoes and put them in a canvas bag and weighted it with rocks and threw it in the river north of campus. At a café downtown he ate scrambled eggs and pancakes and bathed for an hour with the last remaining bar of his father's soap, shaving himself again from head to toe. He slept soundly half the day.

The story broke early Saturday evening. The front page of the Sunday Tribune blazed with the second biggest headlines since the impeachment of the President: UNC STUDENT BRUTALLY SLAIN *Boyfriend Arrested.*

At the arraignment Tuesday morning Barry was charged with battery, kidnapping, sexual assault, rape, sodomy, first-degree murder, and penetration. He entered a plea of absolutely one hundred percent not guilty, a statement his lawyer, whispering in Barry's ear, quickly revised. Barry's parents, wealthy Greeley ranchers, put up the million-dollar bail. Barry is a kind gentle soul, his mother said. As a boy he bottle-fed sick calves and gave them medicine with an eyedropper. My son could never commit such atrocities, his father said. He drinks too much sometimes, but what rancher doesn't. So what if he's underage. It's the cussed laws that are wrong. The state legislature caving into the DOT. If he's old enough to get his ass shot off in Afghanistan, why can't he have a drink?

TV cameras followed Barry everywhere he went. Dozens of news wagons, their satellite dishes raised high, sat in front of the Shay house in Iowa City, the frat house in Greeley, the courthouse, the parents' ranch, The Circle M—M for Mason, the family dynasty name, overnight The Circle Murder Ranch. Urban legends of death cults, mass graves, and human sacrifice sprang up on the internet. Hundreds of bodies were buried in those thousand acres north of Greeley. Disappearing hitchhikers, migrant workers. Prostitutes abducted from Colfax Avenue in Denver.

Friday the Weld County Coroner's office held a press conference. Ginny Shay had been pregnant. Barry was rearrested and charged with a second count of murder and denied bail. Double homicide was automatically a capital crime. Barry became the most famous criminal in America. Seventy percent of Court TV viewers believed he was guilty. He had no more qualms about killing the victim than he would slaughtering a cow, a PETA lawyer said in an interview. Typical rancher mindset. I oppose the death penalty, but I wouldn't lose any sleep if the jury made an example out of him. I'm sorry for the Shay family, but millions of sentient beings are tortured and executed every day in agribusiness Treblinkas across the country, without a pang of conscience, ounce of pity, or any legal recourse whatsoever. Stunned with hammers, electrocuted, cut limb from limb. Pigs are dropped into scalding water and cattle skinned alive. Ask any belly cutter or hide ripper how many animals are still breathing and wild-eyed with terror when they reach his station. His lawyers sued for change of venue. The trial was moved to Denver, where the judge allowed it to be broadcast live.

Tariq spent August and early September shadowing Dr. Dworkin, but found the professor and his wife so physically repulsive he could not countenance killing them from less than a hundred yards away, and since he had no access to illegal firearms, nor the resources to build an IED, he abandoned the idea.

One Friday evening he followed the Dworkins from the Beth Israel synagogue on Reservoir Road to a Citgo station.

Blowing up a synagogue with Venezuelan gasoline would rock the world from Caracas to Jerusalem, from Washington to Damascus, from Tehran to Baghdad to Tel Aviv. He, Tariq, son of a master soap maker, would become a martyr's martyr, among the greatest of the 21st century, of any century, of all time. It would be a Day of Atonement indeed, unlike any the world had ever witnessed.

Tariq shaved himself from head to toe, bathed, and prayed. He drew up maps and with a stopwatch timed the route from the convenience store to Beth Israel. At the library he photocopied manuals on driving big rigs, The Western Star in particular. He would go 1.7 miles, gain momentum downhill and crash into the parking lot and drive the rig and tanker loaded with 22,000 gallons of gasoline right through the front door of the temple. A gigantic fireball of thousands gathered for fasting and prayer.

A week before Yom Kippur Ginny appeared in a dream. Tariq sat in a high-tech strip bar drinking rum and cokes when she appeared through a cloud of dry ice wearing nothing but a frilly g-string and a belt hanging loosely around her neck like a necktie.

Tariq, you filthy dog, you lusted in your heart and loins for me. You strangled me and committed unspeakable acts on my comely body. Stained with the blood of lust and murder, you are unworthy of martyrdom. Bomb the synagogue and you will burn in hell for eternity.

Kafir whore! Tariq shouted in his sleep. You are not Ginny. You are a demon sent to drive me out of my mind.

Ginny danced, swinging around a silver pole. Tariq found himself onstage. The audience was filled with the demented animals he recognized as white American women.

Take it off, sesame head! Shake yo' qutb booty, Muslim whoremonger! Bust a move! Taqiyya! Irtidad! He looked for the direction of Mecca and fell to the dance floor, the stage lights strobing, the pagan dithyrambs pounding the air, throttling his throat, putting his head in a vise of drumbeats urging him to acts and words of unforgivable blasphemy.

O Compassionate, Indulgent, Most Merciful, spare me the torments of this demon disguised as a beautiful woman, white as a worm and soft like undercooked dough, her blue eyes blasted in the glass furnace of the inferno, to lure me onto the glowing coals of the pit!

No prayer in here, Ginny said. She kicked him in the side with the sharp point of her high-heeled pump. He rolled over onto his back. A rib cracked. She straddled him and squatted, the double superabundance of her buttocks smothering his nose and mouth and trembling more and more violently as she climbed the heights of the mad abandon of her pleasure and stroked his zib, her glistening nectar streaming down his cheeks into his ears like tears of grief as he gasped for breath, both of them, mu'min and pagan, together again and again and again.

It was four a.m. He bathed and scrubbed until his skin bled and shaved himself from head to toe. He burned his sheets in the fireplace and at an all-night Wal-Mart bought Clorox and steel wool and scrubbed the stains on the mattress until the fabric disintegrated. He spent the morning on the phone looking for hand-made soap from Syria. He knew his father's recipe and could make as much as he needed, but it would take months to dry to perfection. At a health food store he bought dozens of bars of laurel soap that did not reek too horribly of the infidel and his diet of rancid pork, oniony milk, and bleached flour.

His hands itched madly. That night he could not sleep, tormented by visions of Ginny on stage in a strip club, in a brothel, in a live sex show with half a dozen women, at an orgy in Palestine presided over by Darius' fifth satrapy, when all of Syria was Rome's whore, a century before the birth of the Messenger of Allah and the Seal of the Prophets. He left his apartment and walked south towards campus, stopping at Shuckum's, a sport's bar, where he drank shot after shot of vodka until the bartender cut him off. He staggered back to his apartment and passed out but woke at the exact moment he strangled Ginny for the fifth and final time. In a celestial robe of stars she floated at the end of his bed, her blonde hair flowing in the winds of heaven. He was soaked with sweat and paralyzed.

Protect me from these unclean spirits!

Before you blow up Beth Israel, you must make one final ablution, one bath of baths for the final sacrifice.

Smokeless fire! Mr. Popo. Captain Howdy! Fuel for hellfire. Abundance of rain! Stop the itching. Stop the burning. I'll do anything. Tell me you are djinn of good. Even the devil converted to Islam.

I am Ginny Shay, the girl you murdered and whose corpse you abused. I am come from heaven to send you down a righteous path. Unless you obey you will burn in darkness forever.

What must I do.

Bathe in lye. Only lye will wash away your crimes.

But it will kill me.

Trust in the Compassionate, the Merciful.

At Ace Hardware he bought a bottle of Red Devil. He signed a form stating the purchaser would use it for purposes other than manufacture of methamphetamines.

He drew a bath and poured in the bottle and half submerged a foot. His screams were heard a half a mile away.

He woke up on the bathroom floor. The tub had drained. The lye had eaten through the cover-plate of the plunger. He bathed his foot in Aloe vera and lay down in bed, praying for the pain to stop. He passed out.

You are unworthy, Ginny said.

Yes. I am unworthy. I cannot bathe in lye, therefore I cannot blow up Beth Israel. I am unworthy. Leave me alone. All I wanted was a beautiful white girl. Harems for centuries possessed them by the hundreds of thousands. They were considered barbarians, less than human, true, even animals, but the most prized for the beauty of their skin and the devilish blueness of their eyes. By way of Crimea, through Spain and France, from Circassia, from conquests to pirate ships, hundreds of thousands were enjoyed by Sultans and Khans, Caliphs and

Shahs, Umayyads and Abbasids, Ottoman Turks and Persian Kings. You are all whores, but the most desirable whores of all! Goddamn you all to the thorny torments of hell! You and your Hollywood pimps, blood-guzzling gawwads, spewing vile desires worldwide, over the airwaves and internet, over cables and microwaves, from satellites to relay stations! Raining down despair on the jungles of Indonesia and the valleys of Andalusia, the sands of Syria and mountains of Anatolia. The Euphrates swollen with your bloodlust, covering the mountain of gold! The Dijla dry as desert bones! Your pimps will die, and I, Tariq, son of a humble soap maker, will die a filthy dog, but I will start the fire that will burn the house of war!

In a rented car he waited for the tanker to pull up to the 7-Eleven. It was five o'clock on Friday afternoon. The tanker was a half an hour late. He drank from a pint of Gilby's gin. It tasted like pine cleaner but it cleared his head. His foot, wrapped in gauze, throbbed in his steel-toed boot. The sun would not set for another two-and-a-half hours, but the temple would be thronged with monkeys well before then, feasting before they fasted and prayed.

He saw the tanker pull up to the intersection and wait to make a left-hand turn against the Friday afternoon traffic. He crossed the road and stepping up onto the running board reached into the window and opened the door and threw himself up into the cab.

The driver instantly understood. He reached under the seat but the knife pressed to his ribs brought his hand back to the wheel. Tariq pretended to have a gun in his coat pocket.

Easy now, the driver said. No bullets flying. A motherload of gas.

No bullets? What's under the seat.

A crowbar. We're not allowed to carry firearms.

Not allowed? What a country. You want a drink?

No, thank you.

Take a left but keep going. Then take the first right.

The manager of the convenience store. He'll see me drive right by. He'll call my supervisor.

Let him.

It will be too late then. Is that what you're saying?

71

You are a hostage. There will be negotiations.

You lying sack of shit. I ain't worth a turd to anybody anywhere. You're going to blow this tanker, aren't you.

Shut up and drive.

The driver turned left and then right down a four lane highway past Centennial Park and a baseball field.

Turn here, on 22nd, Tariq said.

Where are we going.

The road crested and doglegged to Reservoir Road. The driver stopped at the three-way intersection.

Get out, Tariq said.

Not on your life. I go where this tanker goes.

Tariq stabbed him in the side, hitting bone. The driver doubling over in pain picked up the crowbar and backswung, hitting Tariq in the head and knocking the knife out of his hand. The driver hit him again and pulled out into the intersection, narrowly missing cars and a van of gospel singers, and put the truck in neutral, letting it gather speed down the incline.

Tariq found the knife. He sank the blade to its heel.

Fuck you, the driver said. He pulled hard right. The truck crashed through a fence and bounced across a field and parking lot to an empty track and soccer stadium of the University of North Colorado. The driver slumped over dead. Tariq dragged him off the wheel. North of Reservoir the parking lot of Beth Israel teemed with cars. He braked and turned left.

Above the soccer stadium Ginny appeared in a cloud of dry ice dancing across a stage lit by evening stars, as tall as a radio tower, shimmering in the high plains dust of the sunset west.

I've waited for you so long, she said. So long. *La ilaha ilaha*, she sang, her sleek legs rising up, honey running down her thighs, her breasts swelling with wave after wave of the milky tide of her pleasure as she thrummed her buzuq, rhyming like a ghazal again and again and again.

Tariq turned the truck back towards the empty stadium, above which Ginny floated, her hair flowing in the wind of the rainshadow, her blue eyes spikes of pitiless ice.

La ilaha illallahu, Tariq shouted. *La ilaha illallahu!*

The truck crashed through the gates of the stadium and crossing the running track dug its trailer tires into the soft grass of the field and flipped over, flinging the cab side over side high into the air. With tools and blankets and coolers and suitcases and laminated maps Tariq orbited the axis of the fall until the cab smashed into the ground. He woke to the smell of gasoline.

The explosion shattered windows across campus and rocked the congregation of Beth Israel, which had begun its prayers only a few minutes before. A fireball flew up a quarter of a mile, turning the red of the sunset into a momentary orange as bright as sunrise. The fireball vanished and left a black cloud and a hole in the stadium a hundred feet deep and three hundred feet wide. Clumps of sod and burning grass and the burning rubber of the track rained down for a mile around.

The police, the FBI, and Homeland Security shifted through the wreckage. The remains of the driver were identified through dental records. What was left of the other corpse lay in a morgue drawer unidentified and unclaimed. In early December an official finding was released at a press conference in the City Council Chambers. An unknown assailant had attempted to hijack the tanker, perhaps with the intention of driving it into a building on the University of North Colorado campus. Evidently the truck driver had driven the rig off course, or deliberately overturned it, thereby saving hundreds if not thousands of lives. The truck driver, who lived alone in a boarding house on the southside of Greeley, had no immediate family or surviving relatives, but was well-liked by his co-workers and the managers of the gas stations and convenience stores where he delivered fuel, drank coffee, and talked about his favorite pastime, fly fishing. A plaque would be dedicated at the rebuilt stadium, renamed in his honor. Anyone with any information or leads regarding the assailant were encouraged to contact the Colorado Bureau of Investigation, the FBI, the Weld County Sheriff's Department, or the Greeley Police via the Tip Line or Crime Stoppers.

Barry Mason's trial lasted less than three weeks. He was convicted on all counts and received the death penalty. On behalf of his son, Mr. Mason sued the city of Greeley, Weld County, and the State of Colorado. His lawyers argued death by lethal injection was cruel and unusual punishment, an insult to the Mason and

Macaulay clans that had lived in Colorado for nearly a hundred and fifty years. My son wants to be hanged, not put down like an animal, Mr. Mason said at a press conference. At the very least let him face a firing squad. Lethal injection is a sick joke dreamed up by federal bureaucrats and ACLU lawyers. It's for crazed pigs and rabid dogs and horses with broken backs, not for a young man sentenced to die for crimes he did not commit. Who killed Ginny Shay? a reporter asked. If I knew, you think I'd be talking with you folks? He'd be swinging from a cottonwood tree with his neck stretched. He's going to hell, that's for damn sure. He knows who he is, and I'll find him if it's the last thing I do.

The case made it all the way to the Supreme Court, which in a 5-4 decision upheld the constitutionality of the lethal injection. The majority opinion argued the state had an obligation to observe evolving standards of decency and therefore had a right to determine humane methods of execution. Allowing a death row inmate to choose the method would open up a Pandora's Box. If a firing squad, why not a guillotine? If the gallows, why not the chopping block, or the hot spit of humility? What if a Muslim wanted to be stoned to death, or an American of Japanese ancestry asked permission to perform ceremonial seppuku and demanded a kaishakunin cut off his head with a samurai sword even before the condemned reached for what is not a knife but a sensu fan? What if a descendent of Mayans or Aztecs asked to be sacrificed to the war god Huitzilopochtli, his beating heart cut from his chest, his body tossed down the temple steps, his thighs cooked and served with tomatoes and chili peppers to a man impersonating Montezuma? What if a masochist asked to be skinned alive? What if a Christian demanded to be drawn and quartered, boiled in oil, or stretched on a rack—his genitals ripped off by red-hot crocodile shears, splinters dipped in sulfur driven under his nails, his toes crushed in thumbscrews—or broken on a Catherine Wheel, or locked in an Iron Maiden, dozens of iron spikes piercing the body but missing vital organs, where he suffocates for days in a horror of darkness and claustrophobia? What if he demands to be crucified along the road to Rome or on a Six Flags replica of Golgotha? Dragged behind a truck or tossed into a volcano? Allowed to walk into the propeller of a Navy transport plane? Tied to a mountain cliff, where vultures feed on his liver, or tied to a metal stake on a Florida golf course, where a ten-mile-long billion-volt 50,000-degree fork of lightning fractures his skull?

Tariq was buried in a numbered Weld county grave, awaiting exhumation should anyone claim what was left of the body or new evidence shed light on its identity.

Two years later Barry Mason was being transported from the Colorado Court of Appeals in Denver back to death row in Canon City when the Corrections van ran over a spike strip laid across a deserted stretch of Phantom Canyon Road. Four men on horseback dressed like cowboys and wearing red bandanas shot the guards with tranquilizer guns and with bolt cutters set Barry free. He leapt on the back of a horse and disappeared into the hills. His father and mother were never seen again. Twice on America's Most Wanted sightings were reported from as far away as Tierra del Fuego.

The Shays established the University of Iowa Ginny Shay Graduate Fellowship in Mathematics. Shepherd of the Hills dedicated a granite bench in the garden behind the school chapel, where a stone fountain of the Virgin Mary bears a memorial, and the cool waters draw canyon wrens down from the dry mountains.

Moon

That was the Sunday 2345.3 misfired, sending a thirty-second pulse of laser light from the Boötes quadrant into PS swimming pool #27, Decatur, Alabama, boiling the aquafied bipeds in an extraordinary six seconds and exploding the tires on all but two of the fossil fuel transports parked in the adjoining lot. It was noted autopsies revealed that under these conditions laser light destroyed all known and unknown venereal pathogens. We voted to further research.

I was called to the Committee Room to give the first phase of report and prepare a statement. Chief Counsel asked me to explain the mishap.

At this point it is safe to assume blame insofar as it is without question our satellite. The cause itself, however, of the minor emission of pulse may be due to nothing more than a sensory overcharge. Static electricity. Thunderstorms are operable under similar environmental stresses. A necessary discharge, unfortunately aimed, that balanced the circuits into appropriate readiness.

The autopsies?

A report I received a moment ago detailed the condition of the organic tissue drained from the recreational reservoir. None of it identifiable, hence no litigious folderol anticipated. One possible explanation is a meteor. Standard debris could be strewn within the hour, CGI witnesses interviewed. Another explanation could be the religio-visionary. Section graph indicates predominate belief in the arrival of a messiah preceded by various marvels, dragons, lions, etc., a zoomorphological menagerie. Holographic imager could superimpose iconography at spooky intervals to connect the discharge with death-fears, shopping hysteria, Christmas good will, and metaphysical horror.

The satellite itself?

2345.3 I am distressed to report is gyrating wildly. The stabilizing jet burners are firing at will, and, as far as we can tell, randomly. At the present rate the satellit will burn through the atmosphere in four and a half days, releasing its nuclear fuel into the atmosphere in what promises to be a spectacular trail of radiation.

Could the explosion be contained?

How do you mean, sir?

A starburst. It's almost Christmas.

Sir, a brilliant suggestion. 'The Star of David.' Bible sales will quadruple.

A messenger handed Chief Counsel a note. After pondering it for a moment, Chief Counsel took off his glasses and rubbed his massive forehead.

I regret to inform you that satellite module 2345.3 has destroyed the moon.

The Poet Laureate, ashen and trembling, excused himself from the Table.

Fuck him, Chief Counsel said.

We all laughed.

Now the good news, Chief Counsel said. A spectrograph has revealed major veins of gold in the fragments now being driven by gravitational winds to the earth. My good men, we shall balance the budget by Tuesday.

This brought us cheering to our feet.

One last item on the agenda, Chief Counsel said. He stood up, arms raised, calming our applause. It seems that someone is going to have to take the fall for the moon. Jones, he said, pointing at me, take the hit.

The inconvenience of appearing in court and testifying before investigative committees notwithstanding, I was pleased to have been selected, for it meant an important appointment down the line. I would be subjected to every scrutiny and slander conceivable, but, like the Phoenix, I would rise from the ashes of my ruined reputation, which would only be destroyed, as it were, on paper.

Meet with our lawyers and prepare a strategy by Monday, Chief Counsel said.

The Attorney General leaned over and asked how I would like to see my reputation ruined.

Particulars are not important, I said. But I'd just as soon seem brilliant as dumb, as soon be perceived as incompetent as mad. Do you see what I mean?

I like that, he said.

'Advertising is maggots feeding on the rotting carcass of capitalism,' Chief Counsel said. Who said that?

Thomas Paine? someone said.

Benjamin Franklin? another said.

Andrew Jackson?

Thomas Jefferson, you nitwit. And what did he know? We'll be as rich as kings. Chief Counsel's eyes glowed. Reardon, call the Oceanic Observatories, the navy, the Army Corp of Engineers, whoever can tell us about the tidal waves and the kind of destruction we can expect. See if we can aim a few at Africa and China. We need to keep the price of gold stable, so arrange to have some of the incoming hit Berlin, Moscow, Paris.

Sir, Haliburton said, my daughter's spending her junior year in Paris.

What a chump. His father bought him a place at the table. But Haliburton's father owned Chief Counsel, and we knew it.

Anybody got relatives or friends in Rome? No one answered. Make it a direct hit on the Vatican. Blame the Pope. Also, we need a way to generate tides when this blows over. Any suggestions?

Deepsea tactical nuclear moon gravity simulators? Reardon said, thinking out loud. Maybe blow a hole in the crust, get a steady stream of lava flowing crossdirectionally against ocean currents. Crack a transform fault. Create massive glacial outbursts.

Look into it. Bishop, make it unequivocally known through diplomatic channels that every last goddamn fragment of the moon is Property of the United States Government. Our flag was still there, up until five minutes ago, and that counts for something.

Let's do lunch, the Attorney General said to me. You'll be ruined tomorrow, but a hero by Friday.

Thank you.

You will be a role model for your people. There is, as you probably imagine, the outside chance you may have to be martyred. Attacked by skinheads. Dropped off in Idaho and left to your own devices. Hunted down by militias. Sacrificed by a coven of witches. After all, they need the moon, don't they?

The Attorney General was stricken with joy or dread, it was difficult to say. For the love of God, what will this do to menstrual cycles? Jenny, get my broker on the phone. To us he said, Are there any women in the room? We all laughed.

Days will be shorter, but how much? Haliburton asked, looking at Chief Counsel, who was now on the phone with his wife.

How many days in a year now? Bishop asked.

I don't care what House the moon was in, Chief Counsel said, the moon is no more. He doodled on a notepad. Why does a planet have to have a moon? He listened to an answer. Solemnly he said, Jones. He listened a while and hung up. I knew then it was only a matter of time.

Chief Counsel lifted his gavel. Recess, he said. Kickballs are in the closet on the left.

We played on the wide lawn until dinner. That night we watched fragments of the moon burn through the atmosphere. Cities were destroyed, some accidentally. The Poet Laureate was struck in the head by a fragment as he raved in a meadow somewhere east of town. His longest poem was a line and a half, but that night he lived long enough to write a stanza. When he died, his post was dissolved. With dark relish born of uncertainty, we anticipated the extinction of the human race. In this way, little was different from the lunar world.

The Valley of Happiness

Sunday morning they left Mannheim and drove east to Heidelberg and sat in Corn Market Square on the steps of the statue of the Virgin Mary. Above them on the hill one of the towers of the Castle was encased with bright steel scaffolding.

Should we go? he asked.

It's why we're here, she said.

They took the long switchback footpath up the hill and sat in the garden.

We should have never left Geneva, he said.

I just remembered it, she said.

Remembered what?

The Heidelberg Man. The Mauer Jaw. Discovered in a gravel pit in 1907. 600,000 years old.

Extinct.

In seventh grade I wrote a report about it.

Is that why you wanted to come here?

Now that I thought of it.

Then let's go to Mauer.

Let's follow the river.

They walked back down the path to the Square and from the Square to the Old Bridge passed The Church of the Holy Ghost. Along the south side gargoyles looked down.

She followed him into the church. Sunlight through the stained glass turned the vaulted stone pink.

Here it is, he said.

Along the aisle at the bottom of a burnt orange and white window was the numbers 6.8.45 and above it the most famous equation in the world.

What does the German say? she asked.

You know I don't know, he said.

At the top of the window an orange arrow pointed down to what looked like a burning earth, under its cracked crust a sea of magma.

That arrow, what does it say to you, she asked.

Hell on earth.

She stood back.

It's a mushroom cloud. Of course.

They crossed through the gates of the Old Bridge. German helmet spikes on white stone towers stood like sentinels at the narrow entrance. On the west side of the bridge was a brass statue of an ape with an empty human mask. The orangutan tail held out a mirror for passersby.

She backed up to the ape and slipped her head inside the face. Look in the mirror. What do you look like.

A particle-smashing primate, he said.

That's you.

Then what are you.

We'll see.

Put on the mask, she said. She took out a camera and took his picture.

Look at his hand, she said.

Which one.

The one not holding the mirror.

The hand was curled into downward pointing horns, a corna.

Heavy metal, he said. Throwing the goat.

The Minotaur, she said.

Warding off bad luck, the evil eye.

But why down.

He's flipping the German bird? he asked.

At who.

Everybody who crosses the bridge.

They drove east along on B37 south of the Neckar River past Hirschhorn to Eberbach. They crossed and recrossed the river several times and though they had no destination felt they'd gotten lost and then found their way south again. Along the narrow valley were orchards and vineyards. Out of the dark wood above a village they saw the towers of a castle. They passed Zwingenberg and Mosbach and wound around the river to Neckarzimmern. Across from the valley on the mountain side of the river was a terraced hill of vineyards that ran up to a castle on a narrow spur. It was late September and the leaves had begun to turn.

Let's stop here, she said.

They sat on the terrace of the café overlooking the river and valley. The restaurant was once the stables. Behind them rose the wall of the castle that led up to the tower at the top of the hill.

Should we take a tour?

Drink? he asked.

A little early, isn't it?

No. But if you won't.

They ate lunch and drank coffee. On the river there were dark grey barges, and a group of canoes and several sailboats. The day was mild and the sky clear but for a few high clouds drifting south.

After lunch they walked through the castle: a pit like a cistern with a skeleton at the bottom, a dusty suit of armor standing in a recess, an iron prosthetic hand.

Her cell phone rang. She stopped to answer it. He walked down the parapet and looked out over the river.

Yes, she said. No. Yes. Good.

It was Karl, she said.

What did he want.

He wants to meet us in Paris.

Can't you just fax him the paper?

I could. Don't you want to go to Paris? I already told him we'd meet him there Friday.

You go.

What will you do.

Drive.

Where?

Wherever the car takes me.

Suit yourself, she said.

He turned away and walked from the parapet to a flight of stairs. She took out her cell phone.

Yes. Karl. Friday. I will fax the paper first. No.

He stepped back out of the stairwell, staring at her. She motioned to him.

Here, you speak with him. She handed him the phone.

Hello Karl. Mike. No. A driving tour. The paper is fine. We're finished. I might after all. We'll be back in Geneva in March. If not Friday, I'll see you then. Would you like to speak with Lucinda again? Adios, he said.

He handed her the cell phone.

Ciao, he said later. What kind of man says ciao. Wasn't he born in West Virginia?

What kind of man says adios?

A man who has to listen to a man say ciao bello and arrivederci.

You've got to stop.

Stop what.

I can't go through this again.

Through what.

He followed her down the stone stairs out to the road and down to the parking lot.

Where are we going? he asked.

I'm driving.

He threw her the keys.

He buckled his seat belt and pulled it tight. She drove fast down the road along the river.

It's an important paper, she said. He helped write it. We can't not give him credit.

Sure we can. The work he did is six years old.

Politically don't you think it makes sense?

Now it's about politics.

When is it not.

Was it about politics when you were sleeping with him?

For Christ's sake, how many times do we have to go over this?

We'd met once. Remember. In Cambridge. Your first year. Dr. Schloss. A party at his apartment over a liquor store. Down the hill from Mass Ave.

I didn't *know* you know you.

So if we don't give him credit, what will he do.

I don't know. Ask him.

He took her cell phone out of her purse.

Buenos dias, Herr Karl. Yes. Mike here. Lucinda and I were wondering just exactly how vindictive are you. You screw your students, yes, but you also help get them published, so if we decide not to give you credit you don't deserve, what will you do? You'll hang yourself? He covered the phone with his hand. He says he'll hang himself.

Then it's settled, she said.

Try not to laugh.

What makes you think I'm trying not to laugh.

By the way, Karl, when we start up the collider, we'd like you to be *inside* the tunnel. Why. Why, you ask. For science. To see what effect the magnets have on mercury fillings.

At Gundelsheim they crossed the river and drove west to Neckarmühlbach and drove south up a winding paved lane to the top of the mountain.

In the inner courtyard of the castle they heard screams from the torture chambers, the rattle of chains and clang of arms and cannon fire. They climbed the turrets and from the parapet climbed to the top of the square tower looking out over the valley. Below a crowd on the castle wall watched two handlers, their left arms crooked and raised up, waiting for two falcons to fly to their gloved fists.

In one of the main rooms of the museum was the display of a herbarium, the wooden library, each plant and its twigs, roots, blossoms, fruit, even its pollen, in a book-shaped box, the spine made from the bark of the species. Along rows of the wooden library in the glass case several boxes were open for display.

Ninety-two volumes, Lucinda said. Impressive.

Besides Karl and me, how many were there?

Excuse me.

Do I have to repeat myself.

No reason to count.

For six years you had no boyfriend. Is that what you mean?

No, she said. What I mean was there were so many I lost count.

Ten. Fifty.

I can count that high.

A hundred.

I can't count that high?

Thousands.

After a while, they're all the same. One smells funny, another has hair on his back.

What about me.

What about you.

He took her hand and they walked back down to the car.

Should we check into the hotel? she asked.

He took the keys and they drove back down the hill across the bridge and headed south. They passed a low modern steel building. On the front of a building were graphics of machining tools and a yellow and black escutcheon lion. It was Sunday and the business was closed. He pulled around back to the loading dock and parked, the engine running and the radio playing German lite rock tracks. The female DJ had a smoker's rasp.

They lay back in their seats.

Not the language of romance.

I'm glad I don't smoke, she said.

Do you have a cigarette?

Ask them.

Six teenagers on skateboards rode into view. He sat up and wiped the windshield with the sleeve of his shirt. Baggy jeans, sports regalia. Chicago Bulls, Miami Heat. She buttoned her blouse. The kids rode up to their car, shouting in German.

What are they saying? she asked.

I don't know, but it sounds territorial. Their Sunday skate park.

They waved. Birds and up-yours.

They look so American, she said.

He put the car in drive. Two of the skateboarders took hold of the side mirrors.

He drove around to the side of the building and floored it. The passenger side mirror snapped off and the skateboarder shot away, tripping over his board. The other skateboarder let go.

That will cost us a fortune, she said.

No it won't. Vandals.

Don't we need a police report?

He stopped the car and got out. When they saw him stand up they paid attention. The skateboarders hesitated and then rode up. He held out his hand. They tossed the mirror back and forth.

He took out a twenty-dollar bill and held it up.

The leader made a peace sign.

Mutterficker. He thumped his chest. His hands and arms went spastic. Bird, gun, shocker.

Mangeras le tas, the man said.

No Amerikaner? he asked.

Waxahachie.

Mexikaner?

Texas.

Buschkuckuck.

The man took out a ten dollar bill folded it into the twenty and handed it to the leader. The leader looked to his companions and the mirror was tossed up like a jump ball. Mike reached up and caught it.

Thanks for nothing, he said.

Fick buschkuckuck, one of them said.

Okey Dokie, another said. A okay. Stick 'em up, muthafuka. Mutterfuck buschkuckuck. Beep beep. One, then another thrust their hips. *Fick buschkuckuck.*

He got in the car and threw the mirror in the back seat.

Fucking psychopaths.

They *sound* American too.

They drove south on B27 along the east side of the river. In the distance they saw a tower and drove through the village Offenau past Mozartstrasse.

Here, she said.

He turned right and drove through farm fields and crossed back over the river onto the road west into Bad Wimpfen.

Are we going to Paris? she asked.

Yes.

You don't trust me to go alone.

I don't trust Karl.

Neither do I. So I'll go alone.

You don't want me to go?

I want you to go because you want to be with me, not because you're jealous of Karl.

I'm not jealous of Karl. I don't like him. There's a difference. I can't imagine what you ever saw in him.

It was flattering. To a young graduate student, he was very charming.

Flattering. You and dozens of others.

That's what you see? Second hand spoils he's done picking over?

Didn't it bother you he had a wife?

You know as well as I do that's not how you think.

Think.

When you're in love.

In love. *In love.*

You were never in love before you met me? Please.

I never felt the way I feel about you.

Jealous? Conjuring nonsense from the past? For what?

Is that what I'm doing?

Should we pull over? Will that get it out of your system?

Worth a try. What is buschkuckuck.

Boys. The best argument I know against Intelligent Design.

He pulled the car into a city lot and parked.

My ex-wife had a moment of insight. We didn't share very many. Lauren was six months old but supply was greater than demand, so her mother had a pump. One morning when she was relieving the pressure, she said, *Now* I get it. Get what? I said. Why men are constantly relieving the pressure.

I don't get it.

Swollen glands. Mammary, testes. Draining the continually replenishing reservoir. Imagine if women in an average lifetime spent six or seven decades lactating. There would be entire industries devoted to its pleasures and problems.

Like human trafficking, sex slavery, and prostitution?

Nothing so depraved, of course. But still.

I see her point. How long did she breastfeed?

Off and on until Lauren was four.

Four. Isn't that an awfully long time?

No, not really. Good for child and mother alike.

Must have completely ruined her breasts.

No, not really.

I'll never do that.

You mean, I'd never do that.

No, I mean, I'll never do that.

I thought you didn't want children.

Too late for that.

What are you saying?

What do you think I'm saying.

I'm pregnant? he said.

No, we're pregnant.

You're pregnant?

He leaned over and put his arms around her.

Is it true.

Yes.

How long.

Seven weeks.

Have you been to a doctor.

One in Geneva. My goodness, he's crying.

No. But if I did, would you mind?

Mike, no. It's sweet.

The collider, he said. Is it safe?

Will it tear a hole in the fabric of the cosmos? Probably not.

Safe for you. And the baby.

Do the math. She, or he, will be born before they start it up.

Have you thought of any names.

A few. Walker, or August, if it's a boy. Zanna if it's a girl.

After your grandmother.

Lauren's taken. But there's no reason to decide now. We've got plenty of time.

Did you know, late in the ninth month, making love induces labor?

I didn't know that, she said.

Something in the semen. I can't believe it. The A word never came up.

The A word. Accelerator? she asked.

The A word. Abortion.

Sure it did.

Sorry about Karl. About—

That's what we do, Lucinda said. Explore infinitesimally small matter.

They walked through the medieval gate across the dry moat and climbed the Blue Tower and looked out over the city to the Neckar River and Bad Friedrichshall in the east. They visited a witch's shop and The Lucky Pig Museum and took pictures of one another in front of the half-timbered Schmuck house and stopped at a bakery with an iron wrought sign of gold enameled grapes and oak leaves. Beside a chalice two acorns floated. Below it swung a golden pretzel hanging by a black chain. At the Guardian Angel Museum they saw lithographs, stone pressings, oil paintings, pendants, postcards, shrines, medals, tapestries, and porcelain figurines.

Any of these strike your fancy? she asked.

Where are the angels of the collider? The superconductive magnets. The Meissner effect. The angel of Paris.

Paris has a patron saint, she said.

What's his name.

Genevieve. Paris has a patron saint, but no angels.

Only devils.

Is this kitsch enough?

She picked up a carved block of walnut. On it a laminated Victorian angel in cloudy robes floated above a boy and girl barefoot on a bridge crossing a gorge.

What's he afraid of, the man asked.

The forest. See the house by the river? In the firs before the waterfall. I never noticed it before.

Before.

You've never seen this before? she asked.

No.

You see this everywhere. The Black Forest. The Guardian Angel. You've really never seen this before?

Why is the bridge falling apart, and not the house? If they can build such a nice house, why can't they fix the goddamn bridge?

Maybe they're not supposed to cross the bridge. They disobeyed their parents, but the angel guides them safely home. See the missing plank?

Of course I see the missing plank. That's the first thing you're supposed to see. Remember that documentary on the Yanomami.

Jesus Christ, Mike. Now?

No guardian angel there. That alligator came up out of the muddy river and dragged the child under. Swallowed it whole. The mother didn't know what happened. A swirl of water and the back of the gator glided away from the bank.

Of course she knew what happened. You think that was the first time that happened? Besides, it was a crocodile.

I wonder how many children fell off bridges. Cliffs. Drowned in raging flood waters of the Rhine or Danube. Torn limb from limb by wolves. Froze or starved to death in the forest.

Christ, Mike. Little Red Riding Hood?

Maybe they're going to a terrible house. Maybe the angel is a devil leading them to their complete and utter destruction. An old crone's house. A witch boiling roots in an iron kettle on kettle legs over hot coals in the fireplace. A gridiron for grilling.

It looks like home to me. Smoke rises from the chimney. Yellow glows in the windows, like the star above the angel's head. I smell bread baking.

We passed a bakery.

A red-haired guardian angel, Lucinda said.

Sweet, he said. In the middle ages red hair meant touched by Satan.

They'd have burnt me at the stake. Should we buy it?

Sure. A boy and a girl. We're covered, either way. We're not expecting twins, are we?

At the Hotel Neckarblick he tapped the desk bell twice, waiting for the clerk, who appeared through a door that led into the apartment of the owners.

Is room 9 available? Lucinda asked.

A panorama view, the desk clerk said. And yes, it is available, for one night only.

Why room 9, Mike asked.

91

It's the best room in the hotel, Lucinda said.

Frau is right, the desk clerk said. You will not be disappointed. The rates are very reasonable this time of year. Have you stayed with us before.

No, she said. Friends recommended it.

They often do. May I help you with your luggage. There is no elevator. The stairs will take you to the fourth floor.

We're fine, Mike said. Can you recommend a restaurant?

The Café Kangaroo. Schnitzel-Mühle. Hotel Tulip at the Rosegarden. All excellent.

Did friends recommend them? Mike asked.

We have no friends, the clerk said, putting the keys on the counter. Only guests.

Goat

do you want more

    no

I'm going to lock up now and let you think about it will you think about it

    yes

if you start crying again you know what I will do

    yes

remember

The door shut and the padlock snapped. He sat in the dark and after a while he fell asleep. There was a stirring, boots on the stairs, a closing door. A tray was put in front of him. He ate without tasting.

    finished?

The tray was taken and the man lit another cigarette. The boy sunk into himself a bit more, feeling his stomach summon enough blood to make him sleepy, but the fear there stopped it cold. He had thought the man meant to kill him but now he knew he would not be so lucky.

    how old are you?

    twelve

    I was twelve once

The boy did not believe this but did not say so.

    do you like football

    yes

    why do you like football

    because

    because why

    I enjoy it

    why do you enjoy it

    friends

    what are friends

The man put out the cigarette and lit another.

people you like

The man coughed with purpose.

people who like you

The cigarette came closer. He closed his eyes, trying to anticipate which eye at the last moment the man would choose. He felt the heat of the ember move from left to right. He heard the man smoke. *there are no friends*

The boy thought about this.

do you agree

He opened his eyes.

yes

how on earth would you know

you just said so

do you believe everything I say

I dont know

what dont you know

much

much about what

anything

how can anybody know nothing about anything who do you think you are, God?

no sir

dont call me sir

yes

yes you will

what

pick

pick what

which eye

The man locked the door and the boy sat in the dark. He remembered a time in junior high when a classmate took to walking around in a black coat carrying leather gloves, slapping people across the face. One day the classmate had slapped him across the face, imitating a commandant in a war movie. He had stood without flinching. Another classmate took up the challenge, however, and that afternoon the boy with the gloves was picked up, held overhead, and slammed to the ground repeatedly, and never again slapped anyone.

Hours passed. He did not know whether it was day or night. He was hungry and peed in a can and drank water. He fell back asleep and was awakened by the toe of a shoe prodding him as if to see if he were alive.

good morning

good morning

did you sleep well

yes

I bet a boy your age likes girls

He did not answer for fear of a wrong answer.

you don't

which girl

any girl

yes

do you have anyone in mind

no

I dont know what you expect

expect

He lit another cigarette.

happiness

The boy sunk into himself.

I dont understand what you are asking me

the very idea

The man reached out and took the boy's arm and put out the cigarette in the palm of his hand.

think about it

He fell asleep with his hand in the bucket of water but it was no use. The pain would pass like the others but he would not sleep well until it did. He thought about her and wondered what had ever made him think that kind of life was to be his lot. A girl like that had no business. He knew she liked him because she had seen it in his eyes, the same he saw in hers, akin to pity, but she did not want to linger there. He hardly blamed her. It was no life at all.

He woke when he was being undressed and bathed. He was half-conscious of cold and warmth and then a freshness like clean sheets. He dreamt as he had many times of flying but always something drew him down.

how are you this morning
is it morning
you do not believe anything I say
should I

The man lit another cigarette.

you decide

The Bay of Drake

We ventured the turning sea, the cold Pacific of an endless sleeplessness of which waves and salt sweetness brightened the night airs of our journey. I rose from my slender bed for the morning watch and left my cabin. A dark mist surrounded the anchored barkentine. I remembered, always, like a pain that inhabits a bodily region, only to infect other corporeal longitudes with tremors of its lingering disease, that my mother, a seafarer of a contrary nature, because she travelled only by land, but dreamed of the salubrious cool of New World springs, lay dying in my father's house beside the gentle banks of the estuary Thames, where the first visionary and epical waters offering my silent tongue a song of distant habitation flowed quietly by, and gave me, as a child, the gift of sleep I now so mourn the absence of, as my story will enlighten only, I sadly confess, to darken there forever, in the reader's gentle mind, so sympathetic, and yet so unlearned of the possibilities of the ways of this extravagant and dangerous world.

Here the sea raged and anointed my listlessness with dreams of my sacred daughter, who survived a mysterious fire, only to suffer her nuptial hour betrothed to a spiritual harlequin, the bishopric's scribe lately suspected of black magic, a mirroring of Scripture with fiendish designs, demon worship of the golden calves. She bore identical twins and died two months after I embarked on this journey, of a fever doubtless induced by her benedict's instruments of darkness, the sackbut, psaltery, dulcimer, and flute, which idolatrous invocations misfortuned my beloved Clementine of divine will, whose elaborations I no longer dare to estimate, but merely follow blindly, a ship cast on an endless and unforgiving sea.

Off shore of New Albion, I am alone, abandoned by my shipmates to the waking dream of my inexhaustible torments.

Where can one initiate, or end, singing of the ocean's depths, icy ecstasies of which few words are empowered to summon their infinite magnitude? When the storm winds die, and the visible confusion settles in to a subtle clarity, the skies in the darkest of early dawn are needled and dewed with incalculable stars, whorls of momentary grace from which I am forced to turn my eyes, as they cannot bear so apparent an intelligence that created the world *ex nihilo*, as the Catholic philosophers have phrased it, for many centuries of beatitude and dreams of redemption, for which they have received only a sentence of death, and a resurrection ever more in doubt, and therefore ever more possible in this world of grave apparitions, intricate longings, and cruel desires smashed on the cliffs and steep banks of this Pacific coast, these profitless shores to which we have travelled, driven by the atmospheric gestures of an obvious and invisible God, and lunar light that falls into the sea like silent and healing transparencies of silver.

Our ship was in immediate need of repairs. During a tropical storm in a more southerly sea the jibs had been ripped from their masts, the sail boom had swept three men to their watery oblivion, and the foretopman, a mere boy of incorruptible goodness, had been blasted from his perch by what we could only believe was the wrathful hand of God. He rose under the screaming wings of the storm and hovered over the deck, his mouth a terrified howl drowned by the roar of the wind, clutching at the airy nothingness that suspended him in its violent currents, and was lifted into infinity. A further plague of despair had descended on the crew, when it was discovered the remaining casks of rum had been poisoned by an unknown and devilishly inspired hand, from which disgusting vats of liquor many of the men drank, suffering violent agonizing visions of Asmodeus, The Prince of Demons who conjured swarms of hornets, she-wolves and lions, leopards and three-headed dogs, where Charon, Boatman of bitter Acheron and the black Styx, ferried their souls to the inferno of Furies, Medusa turned them to stone, and Minos pitched them into the fiery foundation of Hell, where they died of fright on the deck of stinking snows and freezing rains, their hearts seized into one eternal voiceless spasm, and their hands, like claws, grasping at fiends before their unbelieving eyes.

For two months such a pall fell over the ship, a ghost of death and expectation, until the nightmare conveyed to us this bay we have named after our captain, Sir Francis Drake, of London, Albion.

I wrote of the Catholics, with what I intended as a sober regard, since the poisoned rum affords me no other, but I must maintain I am not so universal as they. My name is Francis Fletcher. I was born in Chatham, down river of London, to a merchant of considerable fortune in the seafaring markets of the world, both Old and New, and grew up with sails perpetually before my eyes, which gazed always to the western seas, and which, on my maturation, led me to the vast expanse of the world's unlegended waters. My seminary was Oxford, but my *universality* is the ocean. My father, through favors, secured my post as chaplain for *The Golden Hind*, the ghostly ship now harbored in the awesome and unregenerate Bay of Drake, off the jagged coasts of the New World's westernmost shore. We were laden below our watermark with bars of Spanish gold and silver, gemstones and pearls, four chests of Chinese porcelain later traded to the natives for favors, of which it is my purpose to bear witness to the world the visionary engines of travel that brought us from the froth-worn, broken shore of nipping colds and thick mists, to the city of fallen angels and lakes of fire.

Financed by imaginative creditors in Venice, Pisa, and Genoa, the history of sea exploration is brief, though extraordinary. All of us have been gravely inspired by accounts of Magellan's Armadas, or Vasco da Gama's ships circling the tip of Africa. Less than one hundred years after Pinzon navigated the cowardly Columbus to the worldly paradise of New India, as exotic and untamed as unruly Nature Herself, untouched by the hand of Christian man, Sir Francis Drake became the first explorer to reach these peerless and hostile shores, and I, as chaplain and ship historian, now convey to you our astonishing discoveries.

Though Italian and English adventurers returned to their native ports with tales of the eastern reaches of this vast continent peopled by gentle Indians skilled in the use of their withered hands for the creation of beautiful and complicated trinkets of their pagan ardors, the western shore has revealed to *The Golden Hind* tribes far more dragonish and barbaric, and diabolically disposed to idolatrous carnality.

After days of uncompassed confusion—forces unbeknownst to man disoriented our lodestones as if by the fumes of witchy cloves of garlic, wracked our astrolabe, and spun the dials of our gyro-compass as if the ship were possessed of a malignant spirit intended to confuse and destroy us—drifting and rocking, swept by contrary winds and intolerable tempests, all of us sleepless, dying, and crazed with expectation of our immortal redemption, we watched in amazement that morning a buzzing fowl sweep down, ridden by a creature of

99

indescribable comeliness, a woman who wore only a patchy swathe of brightly colored cloth across her wickedly apparent though remarkably beautiful breasts, which stirred in the crew a whirlpool of Charybdian *hysteria libidinosa*, unclean spirits I immediately attempted to exorcise with recitations of passages from the Holy Gospels. This gorgeous Sycorax laughed and swooped by us several times, apparently controlling the noisy chanticleer with suggestions her corpus mysteriously conveyed to the idiot beast. The men of our ship shouted and raved and stamped on the deck, overjoyed and terrified, convinced some force was now to restore us to our former condition, in which we enjoyed the fundamental pleasures of living in this world, bouts of drunkenness and lust, corporal ecstasies reigned in by moral law, which only made them greater, punctuated by weeping and confessions that scoured our souls, like waves dissolving rock in their fury to be announced as beatitudes of clemency.

She dropped a series of leaflets, which fluttered to the deck, on which were impressed in Omegatype this curious and perplexing advice, which we could in no way decipher:

As members of the Screen Actors Guild, you have been invited to a party at Huey Heifer's Palace tonight. Condoms supplied. Safe Sexy and Enlightened Adults Only. No Hot Lunches, S & M, or Bondage. Only Benevolent and Beautiful and Natural Sexiness. R.S.V.P. Regrets only.

The angry bird swooped so low I feared it would crash into our mizzenmast, already weakened by the violent southern storm, but Fortune turned in our favor, as the woman merely stuck her thumb in the air, and sucked on it passionately, as though she had wounded herself, and was delighted by the sensation of pain. My eyes filled up, brimming with her gorgeous teats.

Thereafter the ship's crew found itself infected by an hysterical laughter, from which I have yet to recover during the days of endless and consuming solitude, though the waky nights are mournful invocations of the events which followed our encounter with the aviary Siren, who in our suffering and delirium we mistook for an angel of mercy.

We navigated *The Golden Hind* by a southerly compass, as the map suggested we must, and launched our dories from the ship for a beachhead of white sand, on which the natives, nearly naked as worms, shiny with exotic and stinky oils, bounced inflatable and brightly colored balls into the air, laughing and grinning all the while for no discernible reason, twitching and convulsing, while other souls cloaked in raven frippery with crazed locks and silver nails fingered their nosepins. One gentleman dead reckoned with a fiery rapier of metal, which blasts mysteriously knocked over his hapless victims, a group of mere boys wearing black vestments and what appeared to be pillows on their feet. Blood leapt from their corpses. The men gathered up the snowy shoes and mounted a hideous horse, whose flatulent roars reared it onto a thoroughfare. We too laughed, viciously, for no reason on earth, like madmen, of whom you do not inquire, Why are you gnashing your teeth and howling with laughter? That they are mad suffices as a *vera causa*.

Infected with this strange magic, we headed deeper inland, which held such surprises of invention I almost am unable to move my quill across this parchment. Iron animals, which drank a pungent cider our navigator's cabinboy mistook for sparkling rum (the poor lad was taken to an infirmary in an agony reminiscent of our liquor insanity and, once recovered, joined us at the stately pleasure palace of Lord Heifer, King of this wild new land), raced mechanically up and down strips of pitch and *terra firma* harder than the cliffs of Dover, emitting choking fumes, wellsprings of the rank density of the atmosphere, in which people, half amazingly naked, ran up and down, jouncing and fondling one another, laughing and screaming as though in a wonderful madhouse in which the agony of excessive amusement is the chief and intended engine of insanity.

We deduced God had granted us a journey through the underworld, for purposes we could not at the moment and I have not yet determined, though the trip left us trembling in the light of divine revelation, which contrary to expectations, is a terrifying, harsh, and glorious transfiguration of the flesh on one's bones into immortal waves of light. I shall record such speculations later. Much later I fear, as my soul, I am convinced by my insomnolent agony, anticipates an eternity in the vestibule where I am presently anchored, The Limbo of The Fathers, where the unforgiven writhe in an eternity of satisfied desire for the benediction of the draconian motions of heavenly revenge, where nighthags moan in the inky smoke of the infinite abyss.

In short, we were all dead, and touring the Inferno, shown by God what pain he had mercifully spared us an eternity of, though some of my companions, I must confess, did not survive the journey into the glimmering shade, but unbelievably as it may echo in the reader's innocent ears, preferred to remain in Hell forever.

We were urged by ambassadors of King Heifer to climb into the darkly shaded interior of one of the giant beasts, which lurched unpredictably, pitching and reeling along the strips of rock, while a violent and disordered noise, whose source we never determined, deafened our ports of hearing. Our cook, an Italian lad of unmanly humours, wept and vomited out the window—which smoky onyx moved up and down of its own will, like the eyelid of a dragon, while the beast itself spewed Plutonian fumes out of sternward horns—crying out for divine intervention in a voice that moved us all, in mortal anguish weeping for the Virgin Mary's benevolent succor in this habitation of Beelzebub.

The beast leapt up a hill and through a gate onto a spacious avenue, at the end of which was an extraordinary castle, and in front of which, in truth, on all angles of which, stood sightly Sirens partially clad, smiling perpetually under the blazing sun, rubbing oils into their voluptuous and astonishing bodies, and gazing round most provocatively to an audience which surrounded them invisibly, for I saw no others but dozens of these creatures admiring one another, who seemed deformedly thin in places, overly large in others, as if their native shapeliness had been disordered by a witchwork never beheld by mere mortals of terra firma, where spiteful Fortune, blind goddess and slave to ignorance, turns her wheel, her foot fixed forever on a rolling stone, but Fortune's vicissitudes remain a toss of the devil's teeth, chancing ill or well, weighed against the woes of this perdurable furnace.

We climbed out of the dragon. Several of the Babylonian ladies approached us, holding their hips, licking their lips so lasciviously I feared I would swoon, or lose what sanity I still possessed. The moral purpose of this erotic punishment escaped me, as I began to feel a desire so powerful it doubtless derived its energy from a volcano, or an earthquake, for as God is my witness I testify the earth moved beneath my feet. One of the women, a black-haired Delilah with enflamed lips of crimson grease, fell into my arms precisely as the master of ceremonies, King Heifer, approached, clutching a smoking pipe and wearing a slothful uniform better suited for slumber than social intercourse.

Oh my *God*, the woman said, parting her cardinal lips. I was astonied. I had not realized this man believed himself to be the Hallowed and Almighty Father Himself, the Creator of the Universe in which even the unbottomed and boundless Pit performs a sacred service.

He put his arm around her.

Surely you jest, I said, buffeted by the winds of blasphemy.

After shock, he said, sucking on his pipe as if it were his very mother's dug. Wow. Did you feel the ground? But don't worry. We're safe. I built this place. Shake, rattle, and roll. He swiveled his hipbone. It's indestructible. I guarantee it.

The irony of these understatements, truth be told, made me inwardly tremble, but I said nothing, and stared at this King of Covetousness with a combination of horror and admiration, for he seemed entirely unaware that he was the mere instrument of a divine retribution navigating his corrupt soul across the infernal lakes of fire, hard and blazing, which we had so far encountered in Hell, although in my seminary studies, I must divulge, I soon discovered the Prince of Darkness, when he appears in the form of a possessed creature, such as a man, or a dog, or a pig, has been known to manifest gentlemanliness, if also remarkable cowardice (a vice of which I feel certain he was possessed, as his bearing showed not a trace of manly valor, since his soul, as it must have been, given his environs, was incinerated daily by the flames of voluptuary mortifications) in the face of even the merest suggestion of a Golgotha's transcendent agony, which I presently proffered by making the sign of the cross over my bewildered heart. The pitch-haired maiden imitated the gesture over her prodigious and mammiferous chest, broiled to a golden turn under the flames of the inferno.

Do I *know* you? a sand haired woman of yet another brace of monumental breasts inquired of me.

I think not, I said, blushing, unable to pluck my eyes from the superabundance of her bosom, the skin surrounding which seemed so taut I feared they might burst before my very eyes.

Who are you *with*? she asked.

Sir Captain Drake, of Albion. I am the Anglican chaplain of *The Golden Hind*. Our modest anchorage is a nautical mile off these wondrous shores.

King Heifer—I say this with little recreational or sporting joy (to which, I dearly believe, the human soul is divinely entitled, with the heavenly safeguards of ecclesiastical law a voucher of good faith), for he truly and self-deceivedly deemed himself a divinity—puffed sensually on his stick of smoke and blew the foul gas into the air with what the fair maidens took to be thoughtfulness.

Monique, he said in a way that made her eyes gloss into pools of winsomeness, these fine gentlemen are with Paramount. They are making a film about a ghost ship discovered in Drake's Bay, north of this lovely city of angels, and we have invited them to our party. Be sweet.

Full rudder, I said, in an agony of surprise and violent sensuality.

You're not, like, the *captain*? asked the woman named Monique. She fluttered her lashes, which I likened to spiders' legs. Dear Lord, I thought, her eyes are green, like verdigris.

If you mean I am not presently captain of my soul, I fear what you say is most true.

You wanna snorkel in the 'cuzzi?

Perhaps on another occasion.

Rain check?

Naturally, I said. I looked up. The sky, dry and hazy, held not a single cloud.

You're different, she said. Not like other guys. They hit on me all the time.

Her poor wayward soul! Not even drubbings by Satan's henchmen had extinguished her cheerful spirit.

You're not the passive-aggressive type, are you?

Never, my lady, I said, bowing.

I had my engrams erased.

Splendid.

Would you care for a drink? King Heifer asked.

A draught of ale will suffice to restore our weary spirits, I said, in a voice I did not recognize. I gestured to my crew, who stood transformed to stone by these bountiful Gorgons, a dozen of whom stood within a rectangle of sand and rapped a white sphere over a fishnet, doubtless a mockery of St. Peter's, when before the Ascension Our Lord appeared and showed the apostles where to cast.

A womanish manservant, who looked at me with such salaciousness I nearly dropped dead of shame—and who wore phosphorescent and incarnadine mouth grease not unlike the ladies'—brought us pygmy hogsheads of beer, within which we discovered an unnaturally cold, thin potation, though delicious to our throats parched by the visible darkness of this hellhole.

He stepped back, appraising my appearance. You look sooo *authentic.*

Yes, he does, King Heifer said, still smoking. Tell me, who is the costume designer for your film?

Film?

I did not at all appreciate this Royal Highness referring to my duds as primordial mire. As a man of some decorum, however, I felt bound by the occasion to answer his impudence.

Sir _____, a London clothier of explorers, adventurers, and gentlemen of the high seas.

King Heifer said—and I here reproduce verbatim his mysterious lexicon—a *play boy* was shooting a *video* of one of his *layouts* in London, and I should have to look him up, for there were many a bodacious *bunny* in Londontown that would be more than delighted to tickle my Saxon fancy.

Whoever this play boy *is*, I advised the deluded man, as my humors were being driven by the hot air of this gasbag from their usual sanguinity to a deadly elixir of bile and choler, ought to do as Our Lord advised: when in Rome do as the Romans do. Hunting rabbits is a fine and engaging pastime, worthy of any gentleman's merry and sporting inclinations, and nullifying a crazed jack rabbit that desires to leech one's blood is a morally defensible action. But one ought, in Albion at least, to be more completely and modestly attired, and not cut lewd looks at every passing subject of the Crown. I assure you, my dear King, I am your humble and faithful servant, but immodest behavior, at least in my country, will not only bring you pain and sorrow, but most likely the rest of your life will be spent in a cold and merciless dungeon at the very bottom of the dark Tower of London, with hollow skulls and famished rats, who in a frenzy of animal nature will raven the very flesh off your bones.

Yuk, the sand-complected maiden said. Now my heart filled like the Deluge with the stormy waters of lechery—proud, base, and so pleasurable as to put me on the metaphysical rack.

Ewe *whips*, the crow-haired damsel said, delighted.

And much, *much* more, I assure you, I said, struggling like Odysseus to resist her lyrical glinting. My heart leapt to my throat and nearly propelled the jelly of my eyes onto her bronzed pomegranates. I prayed the pleasure would cease, hoping the hand of Eternity would apply considerable pressure to my agitated breast and thwart this diabolicalization presently threatening me, like a stand of storm clouds over the dark horizon readying to smash me on Stygian rocks.

Momentarily becalmed, I inquired as to the reason for the royal edict banning *hot lunches*, and what *s* and *m* might stand for, and what on God's bountiful earth *condom* might signify, which questions only elicited unbridled laugher.

We're a classy operation, King Heifer replied, almost graciously.

I swigged a considerable portion of the malt-drink, which amplified the effect of my debauchability, magnifying the enchantments of the flesh aforementioned. Then I discovered I was in possession of a gigantic and inspired will to couple with a wench, which manifestation as a rise in my trousers the women repeatedly cast their eyes upon, until, in a wave of furious, earthshakingly lewd diversion from the contemplation of my creaturely mortality which, as a consequence of my seminary studies, one evening in the pastoral twilight of an Oxfordian April, I had pledged my soul the remainder of my life the eternal abjuration of, I spumed in my breeches.

King Heifer smiled *wickedly*. He had damned my soul, and his bearing was now suddenly achingly proud. He puffed away, as careless as the gaseous clouds which enveloped the city, and rendered it a twilight hamlet of antinomian distinctiveness.

I had not grasped the ideal of what precisely a video *was*, which first word I understood from my apprenticeship to Latin poetry—though they mispronounced it, intentionally, I am now convinced—but every time one of the waking damned mentioned the words in passing, one of Drake's men, a boyish sailor of irresponsible character, moved a step forward, until he stood at a towering girl's chest, his nose buried in the incantatory and hexing cleavage of her breasts. She twittered, as though his nose stimulated an erotic tropic on the considerable cartographical marvel of her body.

He too spumed, and fainted from, I now believe, the combination of aphrodisiacal wolfishness and the plentiful potation, which had us all by now less and less inclined to believe that we were *in* hell, but suffering from a nightmare of bittersweet and overcast and appalled desires, all realized in the flesh of the walking dead, with whom we began to sympathize by witnessing the saturnalia taking place full compass all over the grounds of this erotic inferno.

We were escorted indoors, where, gazing into a large colorful box resembling the eye of Cyclops, we witnessed the torments of the damned imprisoned therein, who feverishly fondled on another's progenitive organs, venomously spat into each other's gaping mouths, forced obscenely shaped missiles and necklaces of beads (the latter we recognized as the sacred trinkets of the eastern tribes described by other explorers, now vilely ill-used in desecratory frenzies) into one another's passageways, all the while groaning with awful pleasure, as if damnation meant a state of perpetual self-deception, in which visible agony became a source of enjoyable torment parading as earthly paradise. I was intoxicated, heady from these fiendish visions, and again discovered myself aroused *in extremis*.

In yet another den of indescribable iniquity a dozen native Africans of the adulterated blood of Ham spun on their heads to the diabolical thumping of boxes in which other damned souls were trapped, who invisible to the world screamed and throbbed in an ecstasy of incoherent suffering. A beautiful mulatto named ****, a pariah from a dark polis on the eastern shores of this continent, said, and these are my words, though the name for this torture was hers, that these youthful unfortunates were writhing and gyrating in what she described as (if I recollect precisely) *hippety hop*—the obstinacy of the Satan's imagination!—which particular contortions she now told me—I almost wept with pity for the hapless damned—were a disorienting Terpsichore called *The Worm*.

I proceeded to yet *another* foyer of infernal design, where doomed men and women, dressed in shiny and taut glowworm gabardine dressings, denuded and bathed in the sweat of their eternal suffering, lay standing, hanging, sitting on various machines of nautical nomenclature diabolically conceived, on which Inquisitor's racks they were tortured by even larger assistants of the Great Satan, who kept screaming at the piteous victims *burn burn burn burn burn*, one of whose hellish attempts at rhyming couplets made me vertiginous, as the great and bloated beast kept chanting,

No Pain

No Gain

which primitive versifying I later decided should be the maxim which greets at the gates the newly arrived into this particular cul-de-sac of Hades.

I am not a man of melancholy humors, and therefore not easily surrendered to womanly griefs but on especial occasions of worldly sorrow, but what I saw next started the molten tears from my face in wave after wave of weeping for the damned turning on these wheels of fire, who as mere agents of hellish manipulation, were now dispossessed of all Free Will, acting according to the whims of spiritual desolation, of which Lucifer is Lord.

A young woman of extraordinary beauty stood before a tremendous burnished looking-glass, before which she was bounced spasmodically up and down and side to side by the invisible clutches of a cacodemon, all the while transfixed as in a somnipathic agony, chanting and chanting in this dark cathedral of idolatries *I love you I love you I love you*, the very deranged chorus the damned were screaming from inside the black boxes in the other chambers of hell, where self-adoration was the vilifying obeisance to King Heifer, prince of this province of darkness.

Torn between these extremes of passion my heart nearly burst. I wept. The beautiful Babylonian lynx named Monique took misguided pity on the sorrowful clapping of my eyes on these riotous manifestations of appetite, as I bore witness to dancing Centaurs and convulsing and scalded she-wolves overwhelmed by the will of God's wrath, helpless and unchaste in the lustreless antechambers of the sulphurous pit, where the racks of Modo elicited cries of impossible mercy, which shapely fox caressed me with incredible knowledge of my riggings and thereby narcotizing my conscience disrobed me and led me into a palatial room of secret waterings, in which a gigantic wooden cauldron of smoky oils sat steaming, and into which she and other she-devils guided me to snug harbor, now a helpless creature before their carnal and imperial obstinacies, which variations defy imagination and enfeebled to this day my capacity to describe them, but which left me nineteen to the dozen cacophonous eruptions later a dazed and damned smiling silly billygoat of a depraved and disintegrated man, unhinged as if I had eaten of the insane, black-rooted, milky-flowered Mandragora dogs rip shrieking from the dungy earth, or Belladonna's seductive nightshade, seizing my reason as its prisoner, immersing me in a Serbonian Bog of unholy desires, where, pixilated by demons from draughts of the rums of Eros, now hardhearted and blaspheming the Holy Spirit, blackened by the resinous gums of Devil dung, and fearless of the wrath of hell's fire, I grew rather enamored of these delicious and eternal acts of darkness, like a woman in love with a donkey, believing it to be a prince, when it is in reality a noisome, willful beast, motivated by stubborn lust and inflamed by a heart filled to the brim with hate, loathing, malice, and every variety of wicked thoughts in a barren garden perceived to be a paradise.

How long the orgy lasted I cannot say, as I lost all orientation of the wasting rhythms of time (and on these pages I neither suckle fools, nor chronicle small beers), because the ardors of Eros are most assuredly the least chronological of sensations, but rather permeable and eternal, invisible currents that washed us to the visible darkness of these shores, spinning and skimming and driving me in passionate confusion to seize every conceivable moment to allow myself to be sailed into ecstasy, but I assume the sun of righteousness rose and set respectfully enough, acknowledging The Father even as I did not, and in an enchantment of rum and lust a lunar year must have passed, during which time I had carnal concourse with over a thousand different gorgeous Aphrodites (Circes, truth be told) my fond heart grew to absolutely adore—we surrendered the entirety of the ship's plundered treasures of silver and porcelain to these dark angels, a mere token of their radiant value on the seafaring markets of the world—as I turned my eyes from the transfiguring light of day, carried on with the ferocity the city of pitchforks enflamed in my heart and loins for an endless single year.

Fearing for my sanity—unaware it was already lost forever—one night I stole back by the light of a waning moon to *The Golden Hind*, where I recounted my adventures to the remaining sailormen, who at first considered me insane, and attempted to shrive my soul to dispossess me of this fit of prevarication, but who, with every detail, in every endless variety of imaginable gynomania and goatish dance of flutes and the wines of the crushed grape, gradually became convinced my story was true, which seafarers then abandoned ship to storm New Albion, leaving me alone on the vast body of water in the last tossing and battered galleon of the valiant English armadas, a flotilla of transfixed ghosts and pirates, the unborn dead whom I escaped, navigating northward to the barren Bay of Drake, solitary with the memories I cannot *Dei Gratia* burn out of my consciousness, nor keep my conscience from punishing hourly with scarifying visions of eternal damnation, forever and forever in a cauldron of recollected desires, never to be liberated from excruciating specter of the neighing narcissi who peopled that pleasure dome, but damned perdurably to the pain of erotic entertainments, on a sea of directionless winds, driven by pleasurable gusts of no earthly compass, to and fro, sleepless and perpetually in fear of the shadow of madness, passing overhead like clouds over the horizons of the sea, water-galls which foretell solely of future storm.

Buy Now, Pay Nothing

He ran into the street on fire. No one knew from what house he had escaped. The martial law as it was written then provided neither sanctuary nor excuse for being on fire. He was shot 78 times, though it was revealed in the autopsy it was a .223 round above his left ear that was the sufficient, necessary, and precipitating cause of death.

Who was he? His corpse was extinguished and kicked up and down the street by the soldiers who shot him. He may have been Caucasian, he perhaps was mixed race, he was not African in any meaningful sense, though he could have been Semitic, if that counted in that day. Perhaps it didn't. Being a Jew, always a liability in most times and corners of the world, had become a virtue for a time, but that era had passed. Was he an apostate Muslim? An Iranian Zoroastrian? An alcoholic nihilist?

Where was he going? Why was he on fire? Perhaps he was frying bacon and the grease lit up the Sunday paper. Perhaps his wife had had enough. We will never know, nor do we care. He was on fire, he broke martial law, he got what he deserved. An unidentified source claimed the corpse, formerly a man, had voted in the recent election. Or had he? He stood in line, he provided a photo ID, he was given a card, which he slid into the ballot machine. Then he stood for two and a half hours and cast not a single vote.

If you can't make up your mind, sir, we must ask you to let others access the machine.

If I don't vote, do I have to serve on a jury?

Are you a convicted felon? Do you own a firearm? Have you ever been under the care of a psychiatrist? Do you have running water, outdoor plumbing, or a vegetable garden?

Serving on a jury is an important civic duty, so I suppose I must vote then. Can you recommend someone?

That's your decision, sir, we are neither allowed licensed encouraged or entitled to tell you who to vote for.

For whom to vote. Who among them is the least criminal?

Sir?

The least gruesome, self-besotted, idolatrous, deranged, and bemonstered?

Sir—

Is there a decent humane man or woman among them?

I—

One that is not a psychopath and pathological liar?

Sir, we do not have to put up with this abuse. Vote or you will be asked to vacate the premises. Remember, this is a church.

This is a church? It looks like an elementary school cafeteria and smells like an army field kitchen.

Sir, vote.

Tell me for whom should I cast a ballot. We're not required by law to cast ballots, nor throw stones at adulterers, especially if they are women, since women are a sore temptation and must be blamed for men's fatal weakness. A friend claims his wife likes him to gently massage—

Sir—

I want to serve on a jury. A capital crime, where I can decide, Life or Death? Which do you prefer?

Sir, vote.

A civil case. An ugly lawsuit. I knew a lawyer once. A divorce lawyer. Nothing brings out the worst in a man and woman like divorce. And to think, they once loved one another, gazed like hammered sheep into one another's eyes while they did the act of darkness over and over and over again. One wife was not only bitter, but extremely angry. It was her godgiven nature to be ticked off all the time. Because of that, and the fact that once attractive she was now homely, single, and will never remarry, unless it is to another homely woman, I can fairly guess her party affiliation. Do you know what she did?

No, sir. Vote.

She let herself into his house and took a half-eaten gallon tub of chocolate ice cream out of the freezer and—

Sir, this is a church.

A church. Since when did politics become a religion?

A Methodist church.

Men are no better. In fact, they are far worse. The less melanin in their skin, the greater likelihood the man is a serial killer, child molester, mortgage attorney, stock broker, financial adviser, sadist, liar, sharper, golf cheat, risk manager, and all around rat bastard, pushing old ladies in wheelchairs into crosstown traffic, kicking puppies, or dashing infant skulls against the exposed roots of ancient trees.

Vote, sir.

I did that once. Why not? It was wartime. I never much liked children in any case. You take the poor forked creature by the ankles and swing round and round just so. Like a chimpanzee did to a five-year-old in that dingbat's primate habitat, the English woman who's daft for animals—

Jane Goodall.

A man discovered his wife was having an affair. No big deal. Happens every day. We succumb to the lower functions of our brain. We obey the laws of nature, we pretty much have to have sex, especially men, all that pressure builds up, day after day, nothing will relieve it—have you considered castration?—driving men batty, wanting to stick their pricks in a warm snug dark forgiving harbor, preferably not a one way street, but that's a question of taste, genetics, history, time, and God, wouldn't you say—so this cuckold, this horned toad, wants revenge. In the prolonged bitter hateful divorce proceedings—am I being redundant here, let me know—his wife has been given their house, but the deed has not changed names. At City Hall he applies for a construction permit, he brings all the necessary documents, he's granted permission by the city to wreck, demolish, flatten his own home. He rents a bulldozer and waits. He waits until his wife is having her afternoon delight—god that song is so shameful, pathetic, disgraceful, a brain worm once you think of that hideous pop song, it's a wonder everyone in the 1970s didn't commit suicide, but since everybody was stoned, who gave a fuck, they knew they'd die soon enough, which turned out to be not a minute too soon—with her boyfriend, a potbellied turd of a human, with a hairy back and blackheads, a goatee and a habit of cracking his knuckles whenever he lusts after the backside of a shopper at the local mall, yes, they're in there, going at it great guns, he can hear his wife's cries, he knows what she likes, she likes it wolf-style, just so, unless the potbellied slob has a bigger dick—this unfortunate thought has crossed his mind, because no matter how big a dick you have, someone somewhere has one bigger—in which case she is probably squatting on his face, since a dick can be only so big before it becomes a logistical problem for the woman, a pain, even. The cuckold cranks up the bulldozer and drives off the flatbed and crushing the white picket fence starts with the kitchen and plows down the table with the pretty flower tablecloth, smashes into the den, crushing the flatscreen TV and rolling over their sofa where they fucked and fought and fought and fucked and drank and fought and fucked for eight and half years. He can hear his wife's cries now, screams really, as she and the potbellied slob hightail it buck naked out of the bedroom into the backyard. The house is not as well constructed as he had been led to believe by the sociopath who sold it to them, she too was a liar, as were his boss and subordinates, but no matter, he learned to live with the endless lies, the agreed upon delusions, the tacitly assented to horseshit, the unquestionable pathological niceties, so many his head felt like a speedbag at the Y, *du bada du bada du bada du bada,* so it is only a matter of minutes before the house is a total ruin. Thank God it was all-electric, otherwise there might have been an explosion from a broken gas pipe. The cops arrive, the man as calm as any man can be when he is in the legal right and has just done something deliriously, morally indefensible, deliciously wrong, provides the paperwork. What can the police do?

Sir, would you please step away from the machine.

But if I don't vote, I can't serve on a jury.

Have you ever been to a doctor? Do you pay federal, state, or local income taxes?

Tell me. A name. One person.

Vote for the dogcatcher. He's running unopposed.

I remember that name. The city found some rather pedestrian porn on his government laptop. A half a dozen women and Priapus.

Step away from the machine, sir.

I cast my ballot. Wither.

The police arrested him and charged him with vagrancy, obstructing traffic, paralyzing a polling place, and harassing a purblind librarian in her early eighties, and otherwise offending standards of decency handed down from one generation to the next, like syphilis used to be, until we had other problems: autism, attention deficit disorder, herpes, drug resistant tuberculosis, a manager class and a national state government bureaucracy as wide and invisible as a giant fungus covering a forest floor.

The man was arraigned and horsewhipped. He cried out against the Constitution, calling it an imposture, claiming the framers betrayed the meaning intent and spirit of the Constitution, turning it into a money-printing machine and the capitol, first Philadelphia, then the swamp called *the District of Columbia*, into a pit wherein gangs of thieves fight over monies they steal from an obedient, hapless, and stupefied citizenry. He begged for the IRS to amend the EZ 1040 to include the following, in this font, if you please:

I would like to receive a cyanide pill via USPS (You are under no obligation to take it, but especially if you did not vote, or if you did not vote, or if you did not vote (perhaps you did not vote), or voted for the wrong party, or did not vote—perhaps you were tired, felt feverish, stuck your head in an oven and realized you haven't cooked with gas since 1977, think government anti-social, draining away the social capital and goodwill of innate human decency and kindness, in order to put in its place rancor, hate, envy, spite, and despair, and want to unburden society of your greedy, filthy, puerile, or senescent carcass—feel free to take it, by all means, you don't even need a glass of water, or scotch, crush the capsule between molars, dissolve it in a cola, sprinkle it on holiday cupcakes (write the Ad Council or the Food and Drug Administration for free recipes). In order not to inconvenience your local health care system, please take the pill and sink yourself into the deepest, vastest body of water available, preferably the ocean. If you live in or near a desert, take the pill and lie down. Chill, you Christforsaken heathen shitheel. The nearest star we call our sun will happily take care of your misbegotten self and the wind sweep away your ingrate dust.)
Yes.
No.

So why did he set himself on fire? His government refused his request for a cyanide capsule. It was good enough for spies and soldiers in the Second World

War, but not good enough for him. That's the best we can figure. In any case, fuck him and the horse he rode in on. We neither encourage nor endorse congress with mammals, fowl, nor beasts of burdens. If you must have sex, stick it to another human. Sex is a lot like democracy: we all want it and deserve to get it good and hard. He or she will hate you forever and you will make a friend you may later defame, or prosecute, depending on your disposition, profession, and where you fall on the income quintile. May we all be miserable and poor together, and should anyone stick his head too high above the crowd, may it be struck off as neatly as an apple from a dunce's head.

Beestings

There was no record of witch's milk. A month before her thirteenth birthday Emma woke from a dream in which she rode a white horse across the sky. She had what she later knew to be her first orgasm, and discovered her pajama top was soaked at each small breast with thin milk. She never tasted anything so sweet.

For a month she hid it well enough. Tissue, panty shields, the thick comb of Kotex cotton, until her mother said, You're not fooling anyone.

Fooling what.

You'll never have big boobs. Quit stuffing your bra. You look absolutely ridiculous.

Mom I'm not.

Like hell you aren't.

She reached into her daughter's shirt and pulled out a sodden Maxi Pad.

What the hell—

No, Mom, I swear,

You're pregnant. How did this *happen*.

I'm not pregnant. I've never even kissed a boy. I haven't even had my first period.

The diagnosis depended on the doctor. Galactorrhea. Hormone imbalance, breast cancer, hysteria. Causes were ruled out: opium, licorice, Zoloft. The milk was tested. It was healthy mother's milk.

Colostrum, one doctor said. First milk.

First milk, Emma asked. It's been first milk since May.

She was excused from gym with a doctor's note vague enough to satisfy the coach and principal. She swam only in the ocean and never far from shore.

What she did not tell her mother, or the doctors, was the unrelenting arousal that accompanied the lactating.

At thirteen she had her first period. At sixteen she had her first boyfriend.

He was a junior, a year older. They made out on the sofa.

My god, he said, taking his hand from under her shirt. You're wet. He smelled his hand.

It's sweat. The doctors call it hyperhidrosis.

It's not sweat. It's milk.

He put his head under her shirt and, lifting her bra and the wet cotton, sucked on her breasts.

Jesus Christ, he said. Are you pregnant?

I'm a virgin, she said.

You're a freak is what you are. A beautiful totally hot freak.

Don't call me that, please. I'm not a freak. Please don't call me that.

That afternoon she lost her virginity, and a boyfriend. She put towels on the sofa and they undressed one another. It was bloody and painful. After five minutes of squirming and thrusting, he filled up his condom and rolled off.

Sorry, he said. I haven't jerked off since breakfast.

Her leaky breasts swelled, her eyes filled with the clouds of an approaching orgasm.

Sit down, she said.

She climbed on top of him. First squeezing one breast and then the other, she had an orgasm of such intensity and duration his frightened cries of *Stop* sounded like groans of pleasure. She passed out.

What are you doing, he said. His hair, his shirt, his face was soaked. He pushed her off and taking a towel from the sofa wiped his face, until he realized he had spread what was left of her hymen on his shirt and neck.

This is too freakin' weird, he said.

It was only later after he left without so much as kissing her goodbye that she curled up in bed, her breasts sore, and cried. But the next morning she was horny as hell all over again.

She bought posters of pop idols, movie stars, athletes and drenched them with milk, once, twice, five times a day. The more she came the more milk she produced. She had fantasies of spraying the ex-president's face, or the entire football team kneeling down at the fifty-yard line under the Friday night lights, while she shot streams of sugary sweet foremilk onto their drooling, delirious faces, after which they would annihilate the visiting team. Then she would unload the hindmilk on the homecoming queen in the back of her mother's Astro van, the queen's mascara like India ink running down her overated face, while the queen still wearing her tiara brought herself off.

When she was a junior at University of Texas, her roommate left a Post-it note on her computer. *You need to see this. ASAP.*

On the monitor her boyfriend knelt down and begged for a drenching. The video had over a million hits. Horrified, she waited for her face to float onto the screen, but it did not. Hands on breasts sent torrential streams of milk into his gaping mouth, which overflowed with the superabundant honey of her glistening teats. He groaned. She heard herself cry out, *oh god oh god*. She had never heard herself come before.

She showered, draining herself into the bathtub.

At the Phi Psi House thousands had gathered in the courtyard for the Annual Bermuda Party. The Spazmatics played Blondie. Emma made her way to the second floor of the frat house, where she found Derrick's room empty. She turned on his computer and found the web site and watched the video. She looked up. A tiny wireless camera was taped to the closet doorjamb.

What are you doing, Derrick asked.

Have you seen this?

I didn't post it online. I swear.

How could you?

I didn't. Please. Please forgive me. He dropped to his knees. I'm sorry. Let have it me with your sweet milk baby.

What, in front of a web cam? Go to hell.

After Derrick she convinced herself she was gay until graduation. She had a half-dozen girlfriends, half of whom were genuine lesbians, the rest like her, sick of gnarly boys and their premature ejaculations, but she like most every human wanted the human touch, orgasms, someone to talk to and be seen with. One butch lesbian, Marty—born Mary—a fast pitch relief pitcher for the UT softball team, which made it to the nationals her senior year—swore the milk made her faster, bigger, and stronger, and demanded a cup a day.

I'm not a cow, Emma said. You're using me.

I'll pay you, Marty said.

Pay me? What do you think I am? Pay me. How dare you?

Emma slapped her.

Marty beat her up.

Goddamn bitch, she said, knocking her down and punching her in the face until Emma blacked out. Nobody hits Marty McDaniel, you got it, you spoiled little bitch with the lunatic boobs. Join a goddamn freak show.

Marty blamed the steroids. The administration suspended her from the softball team, which lost in the final round to Notre Dame.

Emma's next girlfriend was a tall thin English major with black hair and skin the color of chalk. Once a month Jane spent days in bed crying.

What are you crying about.

I don't know. I'm sad.

About what.

Everything. The President—she burst into tears. Rainforests, men, the dying oceans. The Andromeda galaxy is on a collision course with the Milky Way.

That's not for three billion years, Emma said.

I know. And think—we'll all be gone, Jane said, and cried even harder.

Let's go get a coffee. Or take a walk.

The sun hurts my eyes. You of all people, the Milky Way destroyed by the Andromeda galaxy. Do you know what Andromeda means? Guardian of *men*. The road of milk destroyed by the guardian of men. The English call Andromeda the Chained Maiden. How sick is that. God I hate the gods. How could the gods do that to Mother Earth?

Jane, it's a beautiful day out.

Nurse me.

Right now?

Please.

Emma climaxed off each breast, until Jane had her fill and slept like a well-fed newborn, dried rivers of grief and gratitude running down the side of her face, because Jane cried when she was sad, which was most of the time, but she also cried when she was happy, and she was never happier than being nursed by Emma, who found her gurgling and infant grunts of pleasure unsettling, when they weren't gratifying.

Her next girlfriend, Rebecca, had a suitcase of sex toys she gave Spanish names. Eduardo. Juan. Chico. Vibrating metallic balls, strap-on glass dildos, dongs that shot strawberry yogurt down Emma's throat until she nearly choked. The relationship lasted three weeks.

This isn't working, Emma said, wiping her chin.

Harder, Rebecca said. There. That's it. Use both hands. Your tongue right there. That's it.

Rebecca shuddered as if she were having an epileptic seizure. Her eyes rolled back in her head. She gasped for air, swum up from the deep. The seizure lasted for a long time, rolling, subsiding. Rebecca lay still, her eyes closed, smiling.

Thank-you, she said. My turn.

She prodded, massaged, poked, penetrated, twisted, and spun. Nothing worked.

It's only my breasts, Emma said.

That's disgusting. It's so sweet it makes me nauseous. You've never come like normal?

How could I know what normal is. I come well enough.

I mean vaginal. Or with your clit.

I guess not. Do you mind if I take my bra off.

Please don't, Rebecca said. It reminds me of my mother.

Your mother?

Her next girlfriend, Samantha—Samy—was the daughter of an El Al pilot and a Scandinavian social worker. Her parents met in Yalta in the summer months when Watergate was world wide news. In ten years they lost five babies (four miscarried, one stillborn) and flew to New York to see a fertility specialist. Samy was conceived on a spongy mattress in a mid-town hotel and born in Houston, Texas, an anchor baby. The Mexicans do it, her father said, why can't we? Two parents who can read, her mother told her. To them I was a miracle, Samy said. My mother's twin sister became a born again Christian, then my father. A Jew for Jesus. Doesn't that sound strange?

Compared to what, Emma said. I've known stranger things.

Emma and Samy kissed and fiddled, fiddled and kissed.

Yours is prettier than mine, Emma said.

What? Samy said, brushing Emma's hair out of her mouth. My what?

Your face.

You don't like my breasts?

I love your breasts. They're so tender and—

Small?

And dry. So beautiful, soft, and dry.

Spray me with both at once. While I come.

No.

Why not.

A face like yours. Never. If you were three inches taller the whole world would know your face.

What? Some bimbo model. You don't think I'm smart?

You're smart. You know you're smart. Why are you doing this?

Milk those tits on my face, goddamn it.

No.

You did it for other women, Samy said. Men too. Tell me about the men.

What about men. I thought you didn't like men.

I didn't say I didn't like men. I said I despised them. There's a difference. You don't despise men?

No, Emma said. She told Samy about Derrick.

That's not so bad, Samy said.

Not so bad?

Did he hit you?

No.

Rape you?

Not literally.

See.

See what?

Samy told Emma about her first and last UT boyfriend, a soccer player from Argentina who kicked field goals for *fútbol Americano*. Feel this, Samy said. She put Emma's hand on her jaw.

Jesus. What is it?

A metal plate.

He broke your jaw?

In two places.

With what.

His foot.

Why?

He thought I was cheating on him. So he cheated on me, which made him twice as jealous. *Yes*, I said, *I fucked your cousins and brothers and I fucked your father on his cattle ranch on the back of an Angus steer. I held on to the horns while he plowed me like a corn field. I fucked the football team and then the cheerleaders and all of Chi Omega.* He slapped me to the ground. *Chi Omega,* he said, *that's a sorority. That's right, caballero, and I slept with them all. Dyke bitch,* he said, *my father warned me about American women.* The last thing I remember was his leg rearing back. I woke up in the hospital. My mother drove over from Houston. Your father must never know, she said. Why? Because he will kill him. I thought you were Christians, I wrote on a pad of paper, my jaw wired shut. Turn the other cheek. Yes, but it's not *his* face some asshole *kicked*, it's our daughter's, our American *miracle*. How could a man do such a thing? STOP CRYING, I wrote. Dad will never know. The campus police filled out a report, my mother hired a lawyer, the school settled.

The cops were never called?

And lose their star kicker? You are naïve, girl. That dumbfuck football team is worth more to the college than half the academic departments put together. Last year he was drafted in the second round. He's moving to Wisconsin. I hope he freezes his nuts off.

Who was your first woman? Emma asked.

My god, you sound like him.

No I don't.

You were.

Really.

No. After Chi Omega there was Delta Delta, then Tammy and Gwen and Suzanna.

Emma held both her breasts and unleashed a torrent.

Yes, they cried out.

Samy married an investment banker and moved to New York and worked at the United Nations as a translator. One night, drunk and alone, Emma called her.

Do you miss me? Emma asked.

I can't talk, Samy said. Now's not a good time.

When's a good time.

Samy, a voice said. What did I say. What did we agree to.

Is that your husband?

This is Samy's husband, Hank. You must be Emma. I've heard a lot about you. Listen, before I ask you not to call here, *ever again*, let me create for you a once-in-a-lifetime business opportunity.

Business opportunity.

Our L.A. office has a half a billion dollars invested in Time-Warner, Viacom. *The* major players. I'm sure I can get you an interview.

Interview.

With important people in the industry. Start your own web site. The first year alone you could gross a million dollars. Give me your e-mail address—

Samy, are you happy?

No. Am I supposed to be? We have a beautiful loft in Chinatown. On Grande Street. Highest concentration of short sellers in Manhattan. Top floor. Garden on the roof. Below on the street crowds and crowds of people. Dead fish on ice. The men and women smoke and spit. It's foul. I can hardly breath. I think I have tuberculosis.

Samy, Hank said, hang up.

Come back, Emma said.

I can't. You know I can't. You take care, Emma. Don't do what I did.

What did you do. You left me.

I married for money.

Samy! Hank shouted, and hung up.

Don't marry for money. You've heard of a gilded cage.

No.

Don't marry for money.

Marry for what?

Don't marry for love, for friendship, for happiness. Don't marry for children.

For what?

Don't marry.

You're pregnant.

Give me the phone, Hank shouted.

Yes, Samy said. I'm pregnant.

Congratulations.

I want a divorce and an abortion, Samy shouted. Samy and Hank wrestled for control of the phone.

Did you hear me, Samy shouted. A divorce and an abortion.

Don't ever call here again, Hank said. You sick fuck. Join a circus. A side show. Donate your body to science. Join the Peace Corp and feed the world. Set yourself on fire. But leave us the hell alone.

Ten years later, after the plague spread across three continents, and after Emma the entered the convent, she heard Samy and Hank had three children. Hank and the three girls all died. Samy, mad with grief, threw herself on the subway tracks under Grande Street, but the trains had stopped running, so she died of the ninety tranquilizers she'd swallowed with vodka, as did half the rats that fed on her remains.

Emma met Jo at a reception for the Austin Ballet premiere of *Nine Sinatra Songs*.

You look familiar, Jo said.

No I don't. What's your favorite song.

I'm not supposed to say, Jo said. Which was yours.

The ones you were in.

All The Way. One for My Baby. Forget Domani.

The last one. You wore the dark blue dress.

Yes.

Ballroom dancers really don't dance like that, do they?

Of course not. That's paint-by-numbers stuff. In One for My Baby, did we seem drunk?

Not really, Emma said. Pretend drunk. How old are you.

What a question. Twenty-nine. And you?

Twenty-one. My girlfriend dumped me for an investment banker and ran off to New York. I'm lonely and desperate and my breasts are filled with milk and I've never been pregnant.

What are you doing later, Jo asked.

Watching you suck my teats.

At four in the morning Jo came up for air.

125

Feel better, Jo asked.

Yes. And you.

Much. You are a strange girl.

Strange?

Weird.

Is that good or bad? Emma asked.

For three months twice a week they spent the night together, usually after a performance or rehearsal, when Jo flush from exercise exulted in her own well-toned body and, scissoring Emma with her extraordinary legs, surrendered to a deep thirst. She gained weight and lost the role of Ophelia to a younger dancer.

It's not my fault, Emma said.

I didn't say it was. We just need to lay off it a while.

You lay off it.

I can't. Not if you're around. What do you think I am, a plastic Mary on a dashboard? I can't get enough of you. It's ruining my career. I've only got ten years left tops.

So this is it?

I'll call you, Jo said.

Like hell you will. You lied about your age. Why should I believe you when you say you'll call when you lied about your age?

I lied about my age. If someone's rude enough to ask, you have the right, no, an *obligation* to lie about your age. What woman my age *doesn't* lie about her goddamn age? You'll understand this means I have even less time left.

Enjoy it, Emma said.

Fall semester her senior year Emma in the Science Library's Hall of Noble Words looked up from the blue chair where she sat in a corner by the abandoned card catalogues. She had switched her major from English to Biology and was researching a paper on chemotaxis. A young woman fell into the chair next to hers and stared at the Mediterranean Beaux-Arts beams inscribed with quotations soaring forty feet above them.

Do you believe any of this bullshit, the woman asked.

Emma ignored her.

Carlyle, Hooker, Shakespeare. Pascal. Sam Houston. Travis. Robert E. Lee. Pasteur.

Pasteur? Emma asked.

See it in the rafters? *Science and peace will triumph over ignorance and war.*

Those. I've never read them. Too busy studying. *Now rivers of milk, now rivers of nectar flowed.* Who wrote that.

I'm sorry. Am I bothering you. I like the Lewis Carroll. *If there's no meaning in it, said the King, that saves a world of trouble—*

I've got a midterm—

Coffee, or a drink?

Coffee first.

It's Friday night—

I've really got to study, Emma said.

Coffee's fine.

It was only when Nikki stood up that Emma realized how tall she was—nearly six feet in boat shoes. They drove in Nikki's brand-new BMW to Austin Java south of campus and drank coffee until midnight. Nikki was in the master's program of Science and Mathematics Education and worked part-time for a caterer. The car was a gift from her brother, a stock broker.

Half our family's from Austin, Nikki said. Swedish Hill. The rest is German and Anglo. You?

I'm a mutt. Split-level suburbia. Nothing special.

On the way back Nikki pulled to the side of the road and they wandered through Oakwood Cemetery. On the cold mossy tombstone of J.J. Jurgenssen they made out.

A relative? Emma asked.

Maybe.

Without the empty set, Emma said, maybe not.

Empty set?

O with a stroke.

What the fuck, Nikki said. Did you just have a baby?

No.

Emma explained.

Nothing special? Nikki said.

For the next two months they spent every night together, mostly in Emma's apartment. Emma spent the rest of her time in the Life Science library, while Nikki seemed to have no schoolwork at all.

You know schools of education, Nikki said one morning, a towel wrapped around her head.

Don't you have tests? Papers?

Like I said, The School of Education's a joke. I'm not like you.

What does that mean.

I'm lazy. I like nice things but I'm not going to kill myself working for them. Come spring I'll have a master's degree and work eight months out of the year.

What about the caterer?

What about him.

Him?

I meant her. A couple. They started a chain of mattress stores and got bought out. Everybody needs mattresses.

Why not start another chain.

A clause in the contract. They have to wait five years, or move at least three hundred miles away. They had money and nothing to do so they started a catering business.

Does that pay well?

Well enough. Business has been slow.

You always have money.

Like I said, my brothers look after me.

Brothers.

Early that afternoon Emma went to the leasing office of Nikki's apartment complex on Lake Austin and told the manager she'd lost her key. Emma went through her closets, drawers, jewelry boxes. Under her bed in an accordion folder she found packets of hundred dollar bills and check stubs dating back four years. The Landing Strip. The Emperor's Club. The most recent were direct deposit statements from The Yellow Rose on North Lamar. Emma took a thousand dollars and left the folder open on Nikki's kitchen table.

At The Yellow Rose she paid the ten-dollar cover and waited for her eyes to grow accustomed to the dark. Through the cigarette and artificial disco smoke lights spun and women on polished stages holding onto burnished brass poles turned like lovely pink and brown sides of Texas steer under cafeteria heat lamps. She sat at the bar and ordered a glass of wine.

The young barmaid in a Yellow Rose t-shirt set down the glass.

You're not working, are you.

Excuse me?

You better not be working. She pointed to a camera dome in the ceiling.

They'll throw your pretty ass out.

Who will.

The managers.

Have you seen Nikki.

Which Nikki.

Nikki Jørgenssen.

Nobody by that name I know works here. Is she a dancer or a waitress?

I'm not sure.

You're not sure.

Emma showed her a photograph.

You mean Blondie. The Swedish Amazon. She's working.

Where?

The VIP room.

Where's that.

It's private.

Where is it.

Upstairs. Members only.

How do I join.

The only members are men.

Emma downed the glass of cold white wine. Another please.

She sat for an hour and watched the dancers. They were a homely sad stupid looking lot and she wondered how Nikki had fallen for such a sleazy sham of glamour. In the bathroom she put on a swollen mouth of lipstick and unbuttoned her shirt.

At the VIP door she said to the bouncer, I'm new.

Use the back stairs. You know the rules. What's the first rule.

The customer is always right.

No, babe. Cops. Don't get busted.

Busted for what.

You in or out?

In.

With both hands he turned her around. That way.

She felt her way along a dark velvet-lined hall whose painted trim was lit up by black lights. A door opened into a janitor's closet that burned her eyes with lemon-scented ammonia, another led to a steep set of musty stairs. At the top was a room with dimly lit dressing tables. Four women sat half-undressed smoking or sending text-messages or filing their nails. A two-way mirror as big as a picture window gave way to a room of outsized sofas, a pair of long legs without heels belonging to Nikki naked to her neck, and men in business suits, ties loosened, glasses of whiskey in hand, cigar cherries flaring in the near dark, out of reach of the stage lights that lit up Blondie the Swedish Amazon as she stretched like a ballerina one moment, the next her back bowed like a gymnast's, her palms to the floor, the next bending over to let patrons sniff where the ghost of a g-string disappeared.

Nikki, Emma said, what are you doing? What are you doing, Nikki.

She threw up in a trashcan.

Who the hell are you? a stripper said.

Get out, another said.

No drinking on the job, a third said.

Who's Nikki, the first said.

Her girlfriend, the fourth said. Can't keep a secret forever. If Blondie were a tire she'd be what my daddy called *top dollar*.

Don't go in there, another said.

Why would I do that.

Look, she's crying. What a sap.

Nikki, my god, what are you doing.

What does it look like's doing. She's making a fortune.

You people are *animals*, Emma said.

What, and you're not?

Go home, sweetie, and sleep it off. You'll get used to it.

Can't take the heat out of hell, another said.

Better leave before she finishes them off.

Finishes them off.

What do you think this is, a whorehouse? She ain't gonna fuck 'em, that's for sure. Blowjobs only. I told her three months a year at the Bunny Ranch in Reno and she'd have the year off. Three years solid she could retire, or go into movies and be a contract girl.

Contract girl, Emma said.

A star.

Emma took two showers and a hot bath and woke up at seven that evening to Nikki banging on the door. The phone rang. Emma drank wine. Every five minutes the phone rang until the voice mail picked up. When the ringing stopped Emma deleted the messages.

The next morning after forcing down a bowl of oatmeal she walked sweating and dizzy to her nine o'clock class. A black BMW pulled up beside her.

Emma. I can explain.

Explain. Explain what. Where your mouth has been, and how it wound up on me. On my breasts. Stay away from me, you parasite.

You're right. I can't explain.

You're lazy.

Yes, I admit it. I'm lazy.

I thought you wanted to be a teacher.

I do, I will.

I feel filthy.

How do you think I feel?

I don't care how you feel. Nobody forces you. But you choose to lie. Some caterer. Where are you going?

To class. Then to the clinic for a blood test.

What if I'd told you the first night, before we made love on the tombstone—

Made love! We had *sex*.

A pod of soccer players passed between Emma and the car.

We had sex, one of them said. The rest laughed.

Fuck you, Nikki said.

Fuck me? Sure thing, one of the soccer players said.

131

Come over here then.

He spun a soccer ball on his middle finger. He leaned down to the driver's side window. Nikki sprayed him with pepper spray and left in her wake twin black tracks of smoking rubber.

My eyes, the soccer player cried.

Goddamn bitch, another player said. You know her?

No, Emma said, but I hear her name's Blondie. Blondie the Amazon. She works at the Yellow Rose. The Yellow Rose of Texas.

No kidding.

VIP room. She took the hundred dollar bills out of her purse and handed them to one of the players. This should cover it.

Emma graduated with honors in microbiology and NASA, The Department of Defense, the Ford and National Science Foundations, the NIH and the Department of Energy, all paid her way through a five-year PhD at Stanford, where she took personal interest in the development of the mammalian cortex, secretly looking for the source of her strangeness but knowing she'd never find it in genes, neurons, or cells, but wrote her dissertation on protein folding, molecular chaperones, and degradation.

She was a research professor in her first year at the Institute of Meteoritics in Albuquerque looking for signs or remnants of alien life with an Electron Microbeam when the first outbreaks in Asia, California, and Africa struck within three weeks of one another. A perfect storm raged across the microbial oceans, killing tens of millions.

On a near empty flight to Boston, where she was to present a paper at a conference in late August, passengers, pilots, and flight attendants wore surgical masks. By the time she arrived at her hotel, the conference had been cancelled and the airports shut down.

She rented a car and drove north to Portland. Her first boyfriend, her UT girlfriends, Derrick, Marty, Rebecca, Samy, Jo, Nikki, none of them had died or contracted the virus. Statistically at least half of them should have been infected and half of those infections proved fatal. Immunoglobulins in her milk? There was no other explanation, except blind, dumb luck.

In a Portland motel phone book she looked up Rachael, a suitemate her freshman year.

Passing through? Rachael asked.

Passing, Emma said.

I know the feeling. How many have you lost.

Precious few. I've been lucky. You?

Everyone but Kyle.

Kyle.

My son.

You're listed under your maiden name.

I never married.

Neither did I.

Any children.

No.

Come over.

Rachael had a loft over her gallery in a trendy part of downtown. The district was abandoned. Memorials, crosses, wreaths, trinkets, teddy bears, and burned-out candles littered the sidewalks.

There are only three left on the block, Rachael said. A family. Everyone else has left or died.

Where did they go?

Who knows? Away. The countryside. Off to die. To Canada.

Why Canada.

Everybody blames America.

But the outbreak started in China, Emma said.

Global warming. Anthropogenesis. You know the story.

But what if it's not true?

What difference does it make.

They drank wine late into the night. Kyle in his cartoon pajamas sleptwalked into the living room.

I found him in the pantry once, Rachael said. Another time he climbed up onto the roof and fell asleep curled up around the chimney.

Rachael put Kyle back to bed. Emma took off all her clothes and sat on the sofa.

Are you hot? Rachel asked. We don't really have AC. I can turn on the ceiling fan.

None of them died, Emma said. I wish a few of them had. But none of them died.

Emma explained, starting from when she was twelve.

I'd heard rumors, Rachael said. But nothing like this.

Rumors.

That you were pregnant, that you'd given up a baby for adoption, that you were a freak.

A freak. A freak of nature.

May I.

Be my guest.

Later they filled a cup for Kyle.

They slept in, twined like lovers, though they had scarcely known one another, but now, with so many people dead or missing, across the years they felt it was fated they met.

At breakfast Kyle ate three bowls of Cheerios.

Do you have any plans, Emma asked.

Stay here and hope for the best, Rachael said. There is a place we could go. A convent in Nova Scotia. My sister spent five years there. In Sydney. St. Theresa's.

They left that afternoon. At the Newfoundland border she showed five different identifications to support her made-up claim she was an epidemiologist.

It's all you Americans fault, the chief of the border guards said. You destroyed the world with your TV and greed, your cars and oil and shopping malls. You half-cooked the world and now it's rotting and making everybody sick. A merde world.

The Black Death killed millions and there was no America then.

Millions? Is that all? Go before I change my mind.

In the dark garden among the cool stones of the convent Emma nursed the nuns. Kyle played in the fountain, frightening the fish and drowning the water lilies. At night he squashed fireflies and with the luciferin made his face a green glowing tribal mask. By the time he turned sixteen he'd fathered fifty-seven children.

Wabash

In the distance dozens of hot air balloons rose glowing in the deepening dusk. They heard the festival music and drove to where the balloons lit up with candles drifted east over the old office buildings downtown. They parked and took a shuttle to City Hall. Under a checkered tent they ate a pork chop dinner and watched a restoration car cruise. Javelins, Chevelles, Demons, Chargers, Bonnevilles.

Fat pickins, she said.

We ready.

They parted and made their way through the crowds, she to the stage where a group of young cloggers danced, he to the rows of booths along the street selling souvenirs and food. At nine they met back in front of City Hall.

You little squawbuck, he said. That good.

Better.

They took a shuttle back to the car and drove south on 2 looking for a motel. Through Hurlburt and Hebron to DeMotte they found no vacancies, so they drove northwest through Leroy towards Crown Point. They drove with the windows down and she lit him cigarettes. They drove under I-65 and went north on 55 all the way to Schererville before they found a room at the Kickapoo Inn, a run-down motel with a cracked fenced-in pool filled with leaves in front of the lobby, where the desk clerk, a thin man in his nineties, dozed in front of a black-and-white television.

Any place to eat around here, she asked.

Which way you come, he asked.

From the west.

Nothing around here. Not at this hour. Not at any hour.

In the room they drank scotch and sorted through the day's take. Seven billfolds. 783 dollars. They put the billfolds in a plastic bag and out back in the near dark he buried them in the woods. A fence ran along the side of the motel. A dog leapt up and barking madly crashed against it. On its third leap the dog straddled the fence and scrambled down. The dog's bark came at him with alarming speed. He blindly swung the army shovel and caught the dog on the shoulder as it drew up to snap. The dog howled and set off in what sounded like a circle back towards the man, who ran to the motel room.

He slammed the door behind him.

Goddamn dog, he said.

Which dog.

All of them.

You a cat person.

I like horses.

They damn sure don't like you.

Pour me a drink.

Pour me one.

When they checked out the next morning they saw a young German shepherd sitting by the fence gnawing on a billfold.

You come back, the old man asked.

You here all night, the woman said.

I don't go anywhere, ever.

Our first trip in ten years.

Where you from.

Portland.

I was thinking Chicago.

Never been to Chicago.

I was thinking Chicago, Mississippi.

Never been there either.

You see a big German shepherd, he asked.

No.

I'm going to shoot that goddamn dog.

They drove back to Valparaiso in time for the Popcorn Panic 5K and the Orville Redenbacher Parade. It was a good thick crowd, ten thousand backs turned in the same direction. At noon they met in front of the Old Memorial Opera House and Porter County Jail. They had sandwiches and beer under a tent and then worked as a team. He was the stall, or she flirted. They had a dry spell for an hour. She looked at him across the crowd.

Somebody stole my wallet, he shouted.

Dozens of men patted themselves and women checked their purses. By the middle of the afternoon they had thirty more wallets.

In the car they counted their take. 2,497 dollars. He put the wallets in a black plastic bag and filled it with gravel and wrapped it tightly with packing tape. They drove east on 30 and stopped at the bridge over the Kankakee River. They took a lure box and fishing poles out of the trunk. NO FISHING FROM BRIDGE. They found a path leading down to the river. He chucked the bag and watched it sink.

Why is it, she said, the dumber the festival the easier the mark?

All that kid shit. Gets in their eyes.

Popcorn parade my ass. I haven't smelled that much diaper since.

Since when.

Since ever.

He took a pint of whiskey from the tackle box.

Drink.

Have I ever said no.

They fished for an hour and caught nothing. They lay down to keep each other warm. The western sky was on fire, the darkness of night rising in the east, a perfect half-moon overhead.

What's that constellation, he asked, pointing.

The trucker babe, she said, on a mud flap. They fell asleep.

A beam of a flashlight came down from the bridge.

Hello.

Yes. They sat up.

What are you doing down there.

Fishing.

A little late for that.

Sorry officer, she said. She stood up, shielding her eyes from the light. We didn't see a sign.

Come on up here and show me some identification.

They climbed up the path. A State Trooper patrol car sat behind their blue Montego.

He took their licenses.

Chicago, the officer said. Nice town. Where you headed.

Toledo, the man said.

Taking the scenic route, the woman said.

49's plenty scenic.

So I hear.

Why Toledo.

Going to visit my aunt and uncle, she said. Big retirement celebration. He was in the Army for thirty years. Colonel Major.

Major Colonel.

The trooper shined the light in her eyes.

That hurts, she said.

Marines, Army, Navy.

Air National Guard.

The officer shined the light back and forth.

Not safe down there after dark, the officer said. Besides, your car is parked illegally.

We didn't see a sign, she said. Fell asleep for a few minutes.

You weren't at the Popcorn Festival today were you.

The what, the man asked.

You been drinking.

I admit. We had a few sips. Always carry a little whiskey in the tackle box. Good for cuts and the cold.

Enjoy that celebration. I'd say your uncle's a great American. What did he fly?

Nothing fancy. A cargo plane I think.

Airlift wing's in Mansfield.

Don't know much about the military.

It's her uncle, the man said.

How far is Toledo from Mansfield, the officer asked.

In miles? she asked. I don't know. Two hour drive if I remember correctly.

They put the fishing poles and tackle box in the trunk. The officer sat waiting. The man stalled the engine a few times, then started it. The patrol car pulled onto pavement, kicking up a cloud of roadside dust, and sped off, its lightbar flashing.

Prick, she said.

Air National Guard. That was sweet. Think that sold him, he asked.

She buttoned her shirt. Dead to rights.

How far is Toledo from Mansfield, she asked.

How the hell should I know.

Two hour drive if I remember correctly. They laughed and passed the flask back and forth. She lit him a cigarette and he pulled on the road and they drove past Koontz Lake, Plymouth, Bourbon, Warsaw, Columbia City, down into Ft. Wayne, where they checked in to a good hotel right in the heart of the city.

The next week out of muslin and calico she handsewed a chemise and petticoat and a mob cap. Inside the petticoat she stitched a pouch the size of a pillow case. For him she made a denim workshirt and cotton waistcoat and trousers. At a costume shop they bought wide-brimmed straw hats and an Ahab beard. The day before the festival she made a red neckerchief for him and a blue kerchief for herself. While she sewed he slept or watched television and smoked.

This town's as dull as dirt, he said.

We'll make up for it.

He got up to pour a drink.

Little early isn't it.

I could sleep all day watching you sew.

Is that such a bad thing. Keeps you calm.

I'm calm.

Maybe we'll go to the botanical gardens.

What for.

To see the plants.

The planet's covered in plants, he said.

You gave me flowers once. No, twice. Roses and a—

I paid the florist and he drove them over in a truck.

You want your money back?

Every time you sew it's you're like a different person.

I like sewing.

Where's my devil.

She's here. Turn around. She got up and put on her chemise and petticoat. You can look now.

No way José any pioneer woman looked like that.

Thought I'd add a 21st century touch.

Damn.

You like it.

Ft. Wayne, you're fucked.

The morning of the festival they drove to the Concordia Lutheran High School and took a shuttle bus to Archer Park. A girl sitting with her parents across the aisle asked her father if the man in the straw hat was Johnny Appleseed.

No, sweetie. He's just wearing a costume, like Halloween.

Halloween, the girl asked. Is where we're going scary?

No, of course not, her mother said.

The father couldn't keep his eyes off the chemise. The man looked at him. The father blushed and looked at his wife.

Follow him off the bus, the man said.

Too late.

Of course.

Are you jealous.

No.

Remember why we're here.

The park was already filled with people. They moved through the festival, down grassy lanes of antiques, crafts, collectibles, stages of fiddle music and cloggers, fife and drums and pipes, a farmers' market, an orchestra playing a possum trot. Stews simmered in cast iron kettles over coal fires, where loaves of bread baked a dark brown. Tables were filled with fruit pies and preserves. Dozens of turkey legs roasted on spits. Abraham Lincoln gave a speech, a Civil War battle was reenacted. Six-pounders awed the crowds with their concussive power. Roving entertainers passed them: Buckeye 'n Hollow Bones, Don Barth's Old Time Medicine Show, and Johnny Appleseed himself.

Hey you, the man said. Johnny Appleseed, barefoot, stopped.

Yes.

Where are you buried.

Up yonder, he said.

The woman came up beside him.

Rufus, take a picture of us.

The man took a digital camera out of his waistcoat pocket.

Cheese.

You look authentic, Johnny Appleseed said to the woman.

She's real all right, the man said. Mr. Appleseed, sir, what do you think of all the rules and regulations for the festival? I mean, Johnny himself wouldn't be welcome here today.

Who two are you supposed to be, he asked, puzzled by the question.

Nobody. Just plain folk. Pioneers.

Are you part of the festival?

Aren't we all, the woman asked.

What organization.

The Ohio Valley Historical Society. We're here to learn and have a good time.

I hear ya. He took a fat handful of seeds from a burlap bag slung over his shoulder and with a wide sweep sowed it across the crowd.

Planting apple trees. My work is never done. Good day. He turned and let go another handful and disappeared into the crowed.

It's not Mardi Gras, asshole. The woman brushed the seeds off her chemise, which she lifted and shook.

Down your shirt, the man asked.

Where else.

Did you get his.

Of course.

Around one they had lunch and worked the crowd until the festival closed at six. At one point the man shouted, Someone stole his wallet, and pointed at a man who, though confused, checked for his wallet too. They took the shuttle back to the car and drove back to the hotel and ordered room service.

One hundred and forty seven, she said.

You practically looked pregnant, he said.

Almost eight thousand cash, she said.

Think of the 150,00 billfolds we let go.

You're counting children.

There was a knock on the door.

She pulled the bedspread over the pile of wallets. The waiter rolled in a tray with covered plates and opened a bottle of champagne.

The champagne's fine I'm sure, the man said.

The waiter stood waiting.

Oh, the man said. How much is the check.

Give him a twenty, the woman said. The waiter bowed slightly, as if to forgive her her companion. He turned on one heel and left the room, letting the door slam behind him.

Unbelievable, the man said. When did help get so rude.

That was bad?

Not as bad as San Francisco. Remember that.

You're right. San Francisco was the absolute worst.

The next afternoon, a Sunday, they went back to the festival in street clothes.

Let's play it low, she said.

Unless.

Unless it falls in your lap.

They passed Johnny Appleseed several times. He didn't recognize them until he saw them at the grave looking over the fence at the rough stone marker.

Do I know you, he said to the man.

No, I don't think so.

Rufus, right.

My name's Spencer. This is my wife Lillian. We drive here every year from Evansville for the festival. It's among our absolute favorites.

Johnny Appleseed took a walkie-talkie out of his seedbag and said, By the grave.

They turned to walk away.

Wait, he said. Evansville you say?

We've got to go, the woman said. Our kids are on the obstacle course. Time for lunch.

Wait.

They separated and ran through the crowds, as they planned, and headed in different directions. She walked behind a group of children, he made himself part of a family. Out of the park she walked west ten blocks and took a cab to the hotel. He took the shuttle to the car and parked in the hotel garage.

Back in the room they flipped through the wallets.

Here it is, she said. She pulled out all the identifications—charge cards, driver's license. William R. Meriweather.

Who is this guy.

Shit, she said. She held up a business card. *Bureau of Alcohol Tobacco and Firearms*. Ft. Wayne Field Office.

No doubt he is pissed.

They put the billfolds and wallets in the suitcase and stuffed their clothes in pillowcases. In the garage they put the suitcase in the back seat and the clothes in the trunk. He opened a gun case and removed a Desert Eagle .50 caliber, ten clips, and a snubnose .38.

They drove west on 24 past Richvalley and Peru and New Waverly. After dark they pulled over by a bridge that crossed a river. He filled the suitcase with rocks and tossed it into the water.

At Logansport they drove south on 25 through Delphi into West Lafayette and checked into the Hilton Garden Inn West at Wabash Landing on State Street, right on the river.

Seven nights, he said to the desk clerk.

Your lucky week.

Excuse me, the man said.

Away game Saturday. Otherwise you couldn't find a room for a hundred miles.

Who's playing who.

Purdue's at Minnesota. The desk clerk looked up at him.

I was born in Minnesota, the man said.

Where abouts.

Crookston. Down river from Thief River Falls. Near Grand Forks.

The woman kicked his foot.

You don't sound like you're from Minnesota.

Didn't say I was. Born there.

Go Boilermakers.

Thought that was a drink, the man said to the woman.

Drinks, the clerk said. Whiskey, beer chaser.

The next week he hung around the hotel room or online in the hotel's business center read up on The Feast of the Hunters' Moon, while she made him a long linen workshirt, a breechclout, leggings, and a toque.

Have to look French, she said.

Can't I go as an Indian? he asked.

Not with anything I can make. You'd have to shave your head. Wear feathers and moccasins.

Did you know in 1791 President George Washington had the native villages burned to the ground, he said.

Good for him.

Saturday early they dressed and went down to the lobby.

Great costumes, the desk clerk said.

They look authentic? the woman asked.

Very.

Go Gophers, the man said.

It was a bright fall day. They walked to the Purdue Stadium parking lot and took a bus to Fort Quiatenon. Half the riders were dressed like trappers, French soldiers, or Miami Indians.

Are you working the festival, a man in street clothes asked. He sat next to a woman.

Food booth, the man said.

Apple dumplings, the woman said.

Central Catholic? the man in street clothes asked.

No, we're Czech. From Texas. Betsy and Joseph. Pleased to meet you.

I mean, do you have kids at Central Catholic. They've got the Dumpling Booth this year.

Of course. My cousin's son. He's a junior.

What's his name.

Carl. Carl Krabbe.

Don't know him.

And you. Your kids go to Central Catholic?

Did. They're grown now.

I'm sorry, the woman said. I know what that's like.

I'm not. You look pretty young to have grown children.

Married the summer after high school. Little Church in the Wildwood, in Sulphur Springs. We had our twentieth anniversary last July.

Son's in the Marines, Joseph said.

No kidding.

Indeed. His battalion was in the battle of Fallujah.

Is he okay?

He'll be fine. He manned a .50 caliber machine gun. Five hundred and fifty rounds a minute. Imagine what that'll do. Got hit with a RPG.

My Lord.

Shrapnel wounds. He'll be fine.

Thank him for his service.

You already have, Betsy said, just by asking. People think we don't want to talk about it. I say there are worse things than losing a leg.

I'm so very sorry.

He'll be fine, Joseph said. Lost his good eye, though. That's a shame. No more hunting in the Hill Country.

We're just glad he's alive.

The man in street clothes took the hand of the woman sitting beside him, evidently his wife. They clasped hands and bowed their heads.

At the ticket booth the man patted himself down, looking for his wallet.

Must have left it on the dresser, his wife said.

We stopped for gas, remember.

Let us buy your tickets, Joseph said.

No, the wife said, we're going to buy your tickets. I don't want to hear a word about it.

Thank you, Betsy said, thank you very much.

You tell your son he's in our prayers, the husband said.

God bless you both, Betsy said. Drop by the Apple Dumpling Booth.

We will, the wife said. For dessert. After our favorite. Venison brats. You haven't eaten until you've had venison brats.

They went in through the East Gate, past the Hawk Range and Wigwam Village, to the Blockhouse Arena, where a band, Traveler's Dream, played *St. Anne's Reel.* Behind booths over open fires steam from stews rose from cast-iron kettles; the air was filled with the scent of nutmeg, fried meats, salt, and cinnamon.

Meet back here in an hour, the man said.

This doesn't feel right.

Feels right to me.

Not enough crowd.

Never stopped us before.

He's here. I can feel it.

Feel what. Who's here.

Mr. Meriweather. Johnny Appleseed.

He pulled her close and while they danced he observed the gathering crowd. Every third man dressed like an Indian or trapper looked like a federal agent.

We're surrounded, she said.

No we're not, he said. Not yet.

Should we stay.

We're here for the Feast of the Hunters' Moon, remember.

Of course.

No way that dufus tailed us.

He didn't have to. If he's figured out the game, he'll know where to go next.

Over a wallet.

He's a federale. Are there any people more self-righteous, thin-skinned, or vindictive?

Not pickpockets?

At the Military Drill Field they watched the Tippecanoe Ancient Fife and Drum Corps and at the River Camp the Iroquois Singers and Dancers, followed by a Clockwork Clown. At the Artillery Park they sat through a thundering cannon demonstration and a Flintlock Reliability Contest, plumes of white gunpowder smoke rising to the blue sky, and then the Tomahawk competition. Early afternoon they ate rabbit stew and buffalo burgers at a booth in the Blockhouse Arena, where another Celtic band, Trois Canards, sang a song in French. For dessert they shared a cone of apple fritters. With the paper plates the woman threw away the day's one lift.

At the Oubache Valley Frontiersmen Blanket Traders they bought a wool blanket and down by the river lay down to take a nap. Around three they woke to cheers. On the

Wabash River a long line of canoes paddled for the river landing. Flintlocks exploded, children danced and clapped and their parents whistled and hooted in English and in French. Behind the crowd Trois Canards played a jig. In the canoes were trappers and Indians wielding tomahawks and pistols, furs, and bibles. One by one the canoes rode up to the landing, and the paddlers jumped on shore to great cheers.

Look what we found, a trapper shouted.

He and an Indian lifted out of the canoe a waterlogged suitcase. They dropped it on the concrete landing. The Indian unzipped it.

Wallets, he said. There must be two hundred wallets here. Licenses, credit cards.

No money, the trapper said. Shucks.

The crowd laughed.

The man and the woman stood up and shook out the blanket and folded it. At a booth at the central gate they bought straw hats and made their way to a bus that sat waiting to fill up. For twenty minutes they sat in silence.

Should we walk.

Where. This is the only way back.

A white Ford LTD pulled off River Road and slid on the grass to a stop. Three men climbed out. The driver was Mr. Meriweather.

I knew it, the woman said.

How could he have known so fast.

He couldn't. He just figured it out, the idiot.

But the suitcase.

Dumb luck. Ten to one he doesn't even know about it.

The bus pulled up on the road and headed to town. He looked back and saw one of the men pointing in their direction, but the other waved him over to the gate, where they disappeared into the crowd.

Twenty minutes later in West Lafayette, the LTD pulled up behind the bus and followed it into the stadium parking lot.

Single file the passengers stepped off the front of the coach. The man and the woman fell into line with several costumes between them and pulled their straw hats down as if blinded by the afternoon sun.

You see anything? one of the men asked Meriweather.

No.

The woman saw a wet spot where Mr. Meriweather had tucked his sodden wallet in the chest pocket of his blazer.

What next, the other man asked.

Look for a Montego. Late seventies, Illinois plates. It was on the hotel camera in Ft. Wayne.

What color.

Camera's black and white, you moron.

No reason to get hostile.

I want those sons of bitches.

All right. Okay. We'll get them.

No reason to make a federal case out of it, the other man said. Meriweather looked at him.

What are you suggesting, Meriweather asked.

We're burning serious federal man-hours looking for a field officer's wallet and a couple of non-entity grifters who stole it. You shouldn't have gotten hustled in the first place.

You want to go home. Go home. Next time you want to kill the afternoon porking some whore don't ask me to lie to your wife.

We're divorced.

No kidding.

The man and woman went in different directions and circled back to the Montego. They climbed in and slid down in the seat.

What should we do, the man asked.

They're bound to find the car. Best drive out of here. Steady and slow.

He backed out and drove around the stadium to the exit opposite of where the bus sat idling.

They crossed the river and took Wabash Avenue to 25 south through flat, quilted farm country. The sun like a dying fire brightened and vanished. They drove the two-lane country road for hours, passing few cars, with no one behind them. They went under I-74 and after Alamo drove west on 234 and then south on 41, the Dixie Bee Highway, past the Turkey Run State Park, through Terre Haute.

What is that smell, the woman asked.

Sulfur. Paper mill.

Should we go home.

Chicago.

No. Home.

For a while. Why not.

They drove through Shelburn, Oaktown, and Emison, through Vincennes, where they went east on 150 through the Hoosier National Forest towards Louisville. At Palmyra he turned south on 135 to Central Barren.

What are you doing, she asked. We're almost there.

Taking a back road.

This late at night?

I've been thinking about Mr. Meriweather.

It was two in the morning when they approached the Kentucky border.

I'm beat, the man said. You want to drive?

Let's pull off.

Past Squire Boone's Caverns and Mauckport near the Ohio River he turned onto a dirt road that led up around a hill to an abandoned church. In the headlights it looked like a photograph of a building collapsing. He parked the car in back of the church away from the road. They took the wool blanket and a flashlight out of the trunk and inside found a solid place on the floorboards and lay down.

The guns, she said.

What about them.

Get them.

You scared?

Yes.

He pulled himself up half-asleep and retrieved from the trunk the guns and a bottle of whiskey.

Drink.

In ten minutes they were sound asleep.

Before dawn the sound of a tire on gravel woke him with a start. He sat up and listened. His wife gently breathing, a night owl, the sound of the church wood ticking. He lay back down and drifted off.

At dawn out back he stood at a sycamore tree with leaves at the peak of turning. Thin fog sat over the valley where the river ran. An iron fence surrounded a small cemetery filled with old headstones and a few monuments with angels and obelisks. A shiver ran across his back. The cold, the gravestones. Being watched.

He walked stiffly back up the stairs of the church.

Get up, he said, shaking his wife.

What.

They're here.

Who's here.

People.

Are you serious?

Take the keys. Start the car, sit like you're waiting to warm yourself. When you hear the first shot drive like hell straight south. Find a boat, any boat, and disappear.

What about you.

I'll hold them off.

I'm not going without you.

No reason for both of us to die.

Why should either one of us die.

I'm not going back. Plain and simple.

Go to the car, he said.

Or you'll what.

I'll kill you.

Go right ahead.

What's your plan.

I don't have one.

You're clean, sweetie. You'll be done in no time. You won't see me for twenty years.

You really expect to shoot your way out?

Hell no. I'll pin them down until you're clear. Then I'll surrender. Visit me in prison.

Of course. Give Meriweather my best. The prick.

Past the altar she went to a side door and walked to the car stretching and yawning. He heard the car start, and then a bullhorn.

Joseph Eugene Washington. Rebecca Ariel Ross. This is the FBI, ATF, the Harrison County Indiana Sheriff's Department. We have a warrant for your arrest. Take any weapons on your persons and throw them out the door.

He flung the .38 as far as he could.

Are those the only weapons.

Yes, the man shouted.

The Montego engine revved and the tires spinning in mud made a high biting whine. When the tires gained traction the drive and differential clanked and he knew she was gone. He heard shouts and confusion. Don't shoot, someone said.

He lay down and through a crack in the door fired off a clip at the police cars pulled into view. Headlights and windshields exploded. He popped the clip reloaded and waited. The Montego left a vapor trail of sound and nothing more.

The concussion of the Desert Eagle stopped everything. No one moved. He felt the ATF agents, the SWAT team, the FBI, the sheriffs' senses dilate. What kind of guns does this lunatic have? Automatic weapons, body armor. For ten minutes no one said anything or moved. A helicopter approached, hovered, and retreated. Police or a news crew, he couldn't tell.

Joseph Washington, a voice said. You have five minutes to surrender. After five minutes, our teams will treat you as a recalcitrant hostile and take the steps necessary to neutralize any and all threats. A course of action from which you will in no way benefit.

Is Mr. Meriweather there, the man shouted.

Yes.

Give him the bullhorn.

This is Agent Meriweather.

Were you at Waco.

No, I wasn't.

Too bad. What makes you think you can go around impersonating Johnny Appleseed, you stupid fuck. You goddamn federale fraud. Maybe Iran or China or Pakistan will do us a favor and detonate a ten-megaton hydrogen bomb a half-mile over the Mall. Improve civic life instantly. Goddamn lamprey fish. Parasites. Johnny Appleseed my ass. I'm old school American bunko. You. You ain't nothing but a turd with a plastic badge.

You have three minutes.

You know how many of my grandfather's stills you jackboots shot up? You nearly kilt him twice. And for what. Blockade liquor. Fuck you. You liver flukes, you goddamn vampire fish, you destroyed this country, now this country will destroy you.

You have one minute.

Live free or die, he shouted.

A song came back to him, one he hadn't heard in his head or played for years. Thirty seconds.

He burst out the front door of the church and fired. He hadn't spent two rounds before he saw hundreds of flashes of light like stars against a black sky and felt a new, strange sensation. He regretted, then he was glad, he would never be able to tell her about it.

The fusillade rang out across the valley. Smoke hung in the early morning fog. Mr. Meriweather kicked the corpse, and kicked it again.

No, fuck *you*, he said.

Smith, he said, where did that Montego go.

Smith climbed into the LTD and studied the tracking device.

Signal's gone, he said.

Cunt drove the car into the water. Smartest thing she'll do today.

She crossed the Ohio River into Kentucky on a flatboat she found down river. In the distance she heard the first gunshots, then long silence, then a barrage that echoed across the valley and left her in the bottom of the boat trembling.

Outside Brandenburg she stole clothes off a line and at a crossroads hid her costume in a metal drainage pipe. From there she hitched a ride on a pumpkin truck to the Bluegrass Parkway.

I'll guess you'll get out here, the driver said. Unless you're going to Louisville.

Nashville.

What. You a singer.

Not much.

You look good enough.

Thank you.

Thanks is all I get. He laughed a friendly laugh. Up the road a piece there's a truck stop. Say Curtis said to give you a ride wherever you want.

Is this yours, she said, holding up a wallet.

Damnation. How'd you do that?

I sat on it. You left it right on the seat.

I suppose I did.

At the Red Ball truck stop, she said, Curtis says to give me a ride. Hands flew up. Cincinnati, Detroit, Birmingham. Chattanooga, New York.

Bowling Green.

I'm your man.

He was in his early forties, with sharp sideburns halfway to his chin. He wore a Winchester Rifle cap. A man on a horse in a full gallop held a rifle in one hand and a lasso in the other. She sat down beside him on a stool at the luncheon counter.

You hungry, he said.

Starved.

Let me buy you some dinner.

Much obliged.

Name's Tom.

Dotty.

She ordered a country fried steak, two sides, and a glass of chocolate milk.

Quite an appetite. How do you stay so slim?

Sewing.

Sewing. I never heard that before.

So how far's Bowling Green.

Couple of hours.

Who's your favorite historical figure.

Gosh. Hadn't give it much thought. That's it, he said, snapping his fingers. Daniel Boone. No, not Daniel Boone. Davy Crockett.

You buy me the material and by time we get to Bowling Green, you'll have yourself a coonskin cap.

Why little lady, you've got yourself a deal.

He stood up and rapped a spoon against his water glass. Gentlemen, I am now King of the Wild Frontier.

Drivers cheered.

Remember what he said after he lost the campaign for Senate.

Naw, what he'd say. Tell us what he said, professor.

You may all go to hell, and I will go to Texas.

I like that, one driver said.

Hell yeah, another one said.

He went to Texas all right, another said. Got his ass shot off at the Alamo.

Remember the Alamo, someone shouted.

You going to Texas, she asked.

By way of Memphis and New Orleans.

Mind if I go.

Then I want one of them frontier jackets. With the leather fringes. And a pair of genuine moccasins.

You'll have to buy a flintlock rifle.

That'll work.

They finished dinner and after a stop at the Walmart near the interstate drove south in his rig on I-65. It rained.

Those are the biggest wipers I've ever seen, she said.

You hear about that shootout.

What shootout.

Right across the river in Indiana. Some lowlife. Tried to take out the whole town.

What town.

Some town. I don't know. SWAT team made short work of him.

What they shoot him for.

For trying to shoot them. That's the way it works. Pull a gun you're asking to get killed.

Real law and order man.

Excuse me.

Nothing.

You know what's funny though. He come out of the building guns blazing singing an Elvis Presley song.

Elvis Presley. What the hell.

Kentucky Rain.

I don't know that one.
The driver sang a few lines.
I didn't know he liked that song.
Sorry, Dotty, what was that.
Nothing.
How's that cap coming, little lady.
By the time we hit Texas, you'll have whole new outfit.

About the Author

George Williams' stories and essays have appeared in The Pushcart Prize, Boulevard, and The Hopkins Review, among others. He teaches at Savannah College of Art and Design and works as a consultant and writer for Corra Films.